CLAY BRENTWOOD BOOK ONE: STRANGER ON A BLACK STALLION

Creative Texts Publishers products are available at special discounts for bulk purchase for sale promotions, premiums, fund-raising, and educational needs. For details, write Creative Texts Publishers, PO Box 50, Barto, PA 19504, or visit www.creativetexts.com

CLAY BRENTWOOD: BOOK ONE: STRANGER ON A BLACK STALLION
by Jared McVay
Published by Creative Texts Publishers
PO Box 50
Barto, PA 19504
www.creativetexts.com

ISBN: 978-0-692-16468-6

STRANGER ON A BLACK STALLION

By
JARED MCVAY

An imprint of Creative Texts Publishers, LLC
Barto, PA

This book is dedicated to my high school buddy

Sam Howland
1940 – 2015

We hunted and fished together and
stood back to back when trouble arose.
We rode the rails as hobos and saw much
of this great land we live in and through it all
we shared a lifelong friendship.

Rest in peace, my friend

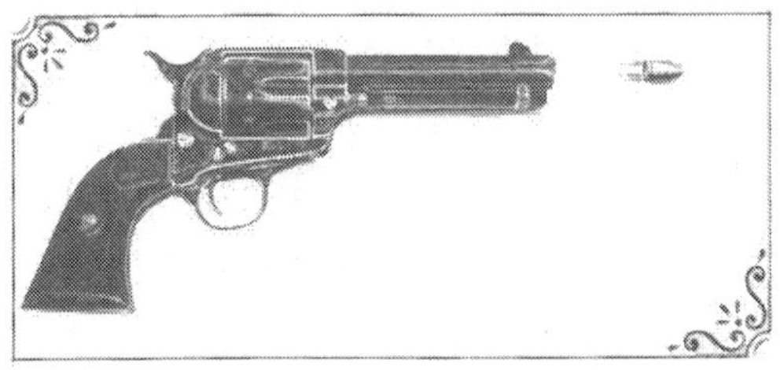

CHAPTER ONE

-

Clay Brentwood saw a small funnel of chimney smoke rising into the sky beyond the boulders just ahead of him and figured it was coming from another soon-to-be ghost town in the Guadalupe mountain range of southern New Mexico, where life was hard. The only things that lived here either bit you or stabbed you with their thorns and left you in major pain. Water was scarce to everyone, Indians, Mexicans and the very few white men who lived in this god-forsaken piece of the world. To many, it was a place to escape from the law because few posses would follow them.

The sun had passed its high point several hours back and was heading for the western horizon, leaving Clay feeling the effects of another long day in the saddle under a scorching New Mexico sun. Near one of the boulders at the top of the long incline, he pulled the black stallion to a halt and stepped wearily from the saddle, dropping the reins to the ground, knowing the big horse would not stray.

Reaching into his saddlebag, he retrieved a leather case that held a pair of army binoculars he'd bought from a retired Calvary sergeant, two years ago this month, for four dollars. The man was in need of whiskey money and Clay was in need of some long-range glasses.

Rubbing his sore back as he went, Clay walked over and leaned against one of the boulders overlooking the small town below. After a moment, he removed his hat and laid it next to him, then wiped sweat from his eyes on his shirtsleeve. Next, he put the binoculars to his eyes and adjusted the distance. The quiet little town reminded him of other small towns he'd looked at during the past two and a half years - sleepy little places with hardly any activity. They were all the same; a few people moving about, while most of the town lounged around waiting for evening to bring cooler air. Then, and only then, would life seem to sprout from nowhere and come alive with music flowing from the cantina and the streets filling with people, laughing and talking and dancing to the music.

These were the kinds of towns the man he was searching for liked to pick on. They were small, off the beaten path, and easy to take control of.

After nearly fifteen minutes of watching, Clay sighed and was about to pull the binoculars from his tired eyes and put them back in his saddlebag when a man walked out of the town's only cantina and stood on the porch. As he watched, the man stared at the late afternoon sky, which was becoming a spectacular sunset. The man stretched his arms high in the air and then reached down and rubbed his back. After a minute or so of massaging his sore back muscles, he reached into his shirt pocket. As he did, he turned and looked directly in Clay's direction. The hair on Clay's neck stood on end and his heart began to pound.

After nearly two and a half years of trailing, tracking, and searching for Curly Beeler, right there the son-of-a-bitch stood, looking around like he had not a care in the world. Curly hadn't changed much; maybe a bit more paunch other than that he still looked like a weasel with a crooked nose and greasy hair. A cigarillo was clenched in Curly's tobacco stained, uneven teeth. Clay watched as Curly pulled a match from his shirt pocket and lit the cigarillo. Smoke drifted off into the hot afternoon air, and then disappeared into the evening sky.

Clay's hands began to shake and he felt a rumbling in his stomach. For the past thirty months he had thought of nothing else but catching up with Curly Beeler and his gang. It haunted him day and night. And now, as he watched, the man stood on the porch of the cantina enjoying a leisurely afternoon, totally unaware of the wrath that was about to descend on him and his gang.

"Enjoy it while you can," Clay said to the man standing in front of the cantina - "judgment day is coming sooner than you think."

The man could not hear him, nor did he have any idea that his life rested in the hands of a man staring down at him; a man he hadn't seen in two and a half years and thought he would never see again, because he believed the man to be dead.

Clay stared through the field glasses to make sure his eyes weren't playing tricks on him. The man's face was burned into his brain and as he matched the image in the lenses with the picture in his head, there was no doubt about it, it was Curly Beeler, the man he had vowed to hunt down and send to hell.

Clay figured he could take up his rifle and send the man on his way right now it would be a long, downhill shot – more than four hundred yards. More like five hundred, and downhill shots were tough. Plus, a shot in these mountains would sound like a canon and would alert Curly's men; and he didn't need that added problem, not now that the search was this close to being over.

Drawing back from the boulder, Clay suddenly felt weak. His heart was beating heavily against the inside of his chest. Finally, after all this time, he was closing in on the end of his chase. The men he'd been searching for were nearly within his grasp. Their leader was just a short distance away. He might be able to shoot him where he stood the truth was, he was so tired he wasn't sure he could hit the man from this distance, and Clay Brentwood was known to be good with a rifle.

Riding down and opening the dance this late in the day wasn't an option - not in the condition he was in. He needed to be rested and sharp when he faced his enemy. He wanted no mistakes. He'd waited too long for this. Besides, to go riding in blind right now would probably mean his death, not theirs. He had waited this long, he could wait a few hours more.

Thoughts began running around inside his brain like a bunch of panic-stricken wild turkeys. Should he ride down and go to the sheriff and try to enlist the man's help? If he did, what could a sheriff actually do, he wondered?

Many of the keepers of the law in this part of the country were sheriffs in name only. They were bad men with bounties on their miserable heads, hiding behind a badge under the guise of lawmen.

Another possibility popped into his head. What if this town had no sheriff? In small towns like this, it was highly possible. And what about the fact that Curly had been standing on the porch of the cantina, acting like he had not a worry in the world? Did he have the little town treed – locked down so that he and his henchmen said what went on and what didn't?

His tired brain told him he would need to check to see if the town even had a sheriff, and if it did, he could size the man up and then decide how to handle things. But, when it came right down to it, he knew he wanted to do this himself. After all, it was his fight, not the sheriff's, nor the people of this quiet little town.

Another significant thought popped into his head. How many men were riding with Curly now? He tried to remember - was it nine or was it ten? If he remembered correctly, Curly had nine hardened gunslingers who would shoot down man, woman or child; it made no difference to them. They were the kind of men who had come west just two steps ahead of the law; men who had no compassion or mercy with anyone who got in their way.

When it came right down to it, the only thing Clay would have on his side would be surprise - but would that be enough? What should his plan of attack be? Should he just ride in with his guns blazing or should he ride in and take things as they came?

What if Curly knew he was being followed and had entrenched himself and his men in the small town so that any battle they might find themselves in would be one sided in Curly's favor? It sounded like the kind of thing Curly would do.

Along with these thoughts and many others, the fact that night would soon be upon him caused Clay to make his first decision. He decided he would wait for morning before bringing his chase to a close. He sorely needed food and rest. He needed a clear head for what he was about to do. Come morning, when he was rested and could think straight, he would come to terms with how to deal with the situation. Clay doubted if they would be going anywhere this late in the day and he wanted no surprises from darkened corners.

Clay knew people would say he was crazy for what he was about to do he had no choice - he'd made a promise to his wife and to himself. The hatred for Curly Beeler and them that rode with him had been powerful enough to keep him on the hunt for these past two and a half years. And now that he'd found them, there would be no turning back. Besides, turning tail when faced with danger was not in his nature.

He was not the law, nor did he have any paper on Curly and his gang. What he did have was two and a half years of pent up hatred, hurt and pain that had festered into a rage that only their deaths could satisfy.

Just then his stomach grumbled. He hadn't eaten anything since early morning, and then it was just leftover biscuits and burned bacon, chased down with a cup of coffee from the night before. For reasons he hadn't clearly understood, he'd felt anxious to get on the trail this morning, and now he understood why. Out here, a man learned to listen to that little voice inside. The one he didn't always understand rarely argued with. That little voice had saved his neck more than once - only this time it was leading him straight into the hubs of hell and a strong chance of being killed.

Clay stepped into the saddle and rode around, looking for a good spot to camp for the night. Within five minutes, he found what he was looking for, though he'd almost missed it.

The place was an overhang jutting out from the mountain. Surrounding boulders, that would allow him to build a small fire that couldn't be seen until you were right on top of it, protected the place. The place would also shelter him and his horse from the rain, should there be any, which was highly unlikely this time of year.

Within the small area, there was a patch of scrub grass and a small lick of water that seeped from a tiny crack in the mountain. The black stallion would be able to get what nourishment he needed and Clay could get the rest his body was so desperately crying out for.

In less than thirty minutes, the big horse had been stripped of the saddle and bridle that had no bit – more of a halter than a bridle. Clay didn't believe in bits and had trained the big stallion without one. He rubbed his horse down with a piece of burlap he kept for that purpose and then turned him out for the night, knowing the horse would not stray from his food and water, nor his man-friend.

A smokeless fire of very dry wood, surrounded by a ring of rocks, was filling the area with warmth. A small pot of beef jerky and beans, along with a pot of fresh coffee hung from a metal rod that angled out over the flames. Clay was too tired to make biscuits. The months of anger had finally caught up to him. He just wanted to eat, drink a little coffee, and then get some much-needed rest.

Within the circle of heat, Clay laid out his bedroll using his saddle for a pillow. A canvas ground sheet over the top of some dried grass made a comfortable place to sleep with the other half of the canvas folded over the wool blanket he would sleep under. Even though the days were scorching hot, the nights could be, and usually did get cold here in the mountains. The canvas cover would stave off the cold and any frost that might accumulate.

Rolled up in his blanket within the circle of heat, he would be comfortable. The big stallion, being shy of critters and people, would alert him to anything or anyone who might come prowling around.

The beef and beans were ready about the same time the coffee was. Clay filled a tin plate, and after crumbling a dried pepper over the top, he set it to the side. Next, he filled a tin cup with coffee and sat down, leaning his back against the boulder so he could be comfortable while he ate.

The beans and beef tasted good, especially with the crushed pepper mixed in for flavoring. An old Mexican man he'd met just after moving to Texas from southeastern Kansas taught him about using dried peppers for seasoning, and from then on there was always a small bag of the fiery little jalapenos tucked into his saddlebag.

He attacked his meal like a starved wolf in a hen house and then cleaned out the small pot, giving him a second helping, which he ate more slowly.

As he ate, a little of the anxiety and worry he'd been carrying around felt like it was being lifted - not a whole lot just enough so that he could feel the difference.

Before he could be totally free of the burden he carried, he still had tomorrow to deal with, and it would be anybody's guess how that would turn out. Clay knew Curly Beeler and his gang would not just lie down and die because he pointed a gun at them. They'd had their own way far too long. For the past several years, Curly and his bunch had run roughshod over many a small town and several ranches in Kansas, Oklahoma, and Texas, along with a good share of the southern part of the New Mexico Territory.

The Texas Rangers sent three rangers to arrest Curly and the men who rode with him. If possible, they were to bring them back alive, to be hung if that was not possible then they had the authority to put lead into them. The three rangers were never seen or heard of again. They had simply disappeared. It was believed that Curly and his bunch had done them in since no bodies had been found as evidence, Curly and his men had never been officially charged with their deaths.

In reality, this was the way Clay preferred to do it – standing toe to toe with the devil; facing him and his men down in front of the whole town, and no man accusing him of being a back shooter or asking for help.

There was no doubt it had been the anger in his heart that had kept him in the hunt these past thirty months. And now the chase was coming to a close. Tomorrow it would be over, one way or another. Either they would be dead or he would.

The honest truth was, he didn't want to see them turned over to the law where they might somehow be released due to some technicality, whereby he would have to start the hunt all over again.

He had been not only the victim but also the witness to their crimes and now he would be the judge and jury along with being the executioner. He figured in his heart, it was his right. He had earned it. He'd been raised to abide by the law. And basically, he was a peace-loving man who went out of his way to avoid a fight; always trying to help folks in need - but this was different. These men were viler than a pack of bloodthirsty wolves. They killed without reason and laughed at their dying victims. Scum like this didn't deserve to live.

After supper, he used water seeping from the rock to clean up his utensils, and then sat them next to the fire to dry.

He poured himself another cup of coffee and once more leaned back against the boulder. Clay rolled a cigarette and lit it with the hot end of a stick he took from the fire. He blew a smoke ring into the air and then reached into his saddlebag and pulled out an old friend who had been with him for some time now; a copy of Leo Tolstoy's War and Peace, which he'd already read several times. It was one of two books he carried with him. The other was a lively story about a young boy named Tom Sawyer, written by a fella by the name of Mark Twain. Both stories were totally different in context each one allowed him to escape from his day-to-day trials and tribulations. Reading material was scarce and he valued what little he had.

Tomorrow there would be hell to pay tonight he would escape in his book for a little while, and when he got too tired to read, he would get some much-needed rest.

Coffee didn't keep Clay awake like it did a lot of folks after reading only a few chapters - his eyelids began to get heavy. Laying the book aside, he looked up at the night sky. The moon was close to its zenith and Clay decided it was time to call it a day. Standing up with a groan, his tired and aching joints crying out in pain, he returned his book to its place in the saddlebag.

Next, he stretched, walked over to the fire and set the coffee pot off to the side, then added more fuel to the fire before climbing under the blanket and canvas covering that would keep out the cold night air -

knowing the black stallion would alert him should anyone or anything come prowling around.

Somewhere around two in the morning, Clay crawled out of his warm bed and walked off away from the camp to relieve himself, the cold air biting at any uncovered body parts. As he stood looking up at the night sky, Clay marveled at the amount of stars there were, and once again wondered to himself if somewhere up there among all those twinkling lights, was there another world just like this one, and was there a man, maybe just like him, staring at the sky, wondering the same thing he was? Life was full of mysterious things far beyond his comprehension.

When he finished his business, he threw his extra blanket over the black stallion's back to help keep him warm. It was turning out to be a cold night. Clay added more wood to the fire before snuggling back into his warm bed. Daylight was only a few hours away and he figured he would need all the rest he could get.

Clearing his mind and allowing it to be free of thoughts so he could sleep at night was something he had taught himself to do, which allowed him to sleep even when he had a troubled mind. The world and all of his problems would always be there the next day, so there was no use losing sleep by worrying about them. A few minutes later, snoring could be heard coming from beneath his hat.

That night, as cold weather settled over the land, Clay dreamed about a giant catfish that made its home in the muddy waters of the Arkansas River that ran next to the small town where he'd grown up. The huge catfish had drowned his best friend Sam Howland, when Sam was trying to lug him ashore and got his hand caught in the fish's mouth. The fish had bitten down and dragged Sam to the bottom of the river. The day of Sam's funeral, Clay had sworn revenge.

Many men had tried to catch the monster fish it was Clay Brentwood, at the ripe old age of sixteen who had tied a big knife to his hand and dove into the muddy water of the sinkhole where the fish liked to hide.

For years people talked about how Clay almost lost his life that day. People who had witnessed the event said Clay would drag the big fish to the surface and grab a small amount of air before the fish pulled him back down. Six times the monster catfish took Clay to the bottom before Clay finally won the fight and dragged the bloody carcass to the shore, where several of the townsmen put gaffs into the giant fish and hauled him onto the bank.

That day, Clay Brentwood's name went down in the local history books. The monster fish weighed one hundred twenty-two pounds; a record size flathead catfish if ever there was one. Someone cut off the fish's head and mounted it on a piece of plank board and hung it over the front door of Macmillan's mercantile store. They hung a sign below with the tale of Clay's revenge for his best friend's death, written on a large piece of pine.

For as long as he lived there, people still patted him on the back and talked about the day he dove into the sinkhole after the giant flathead catfish. It finally got to the point where Clay would sneak off down an alley when he saw people heading his way.

Clay hadn't been looking for glory that day and he didn't like standin' around talking about it. He had wanted revenge for what the giant fish did to his best friend. That was it, plain and simple. Even as he dove into the river, he knew killing the giant fish would not bring his friend back, it would only satisfy the revenge that raged inside him. But as the good book said, "An eye for an eye and a tooth for a tooth."

To Clay, this seemed like pretty much the same thing. Killing Curly and his gang would not remove the hurt in his heart; nor would it bring his wife back. The deaths of these outlaws would only satisfy the revenge his heart cried out for.

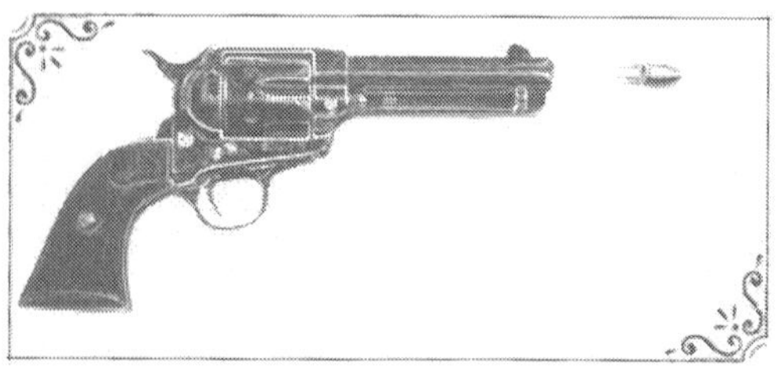

CHAPTER TWO

-

A beam of sunlight wormed its way beneath the canvas and blanket and drove itself into Clay's left eye, bringing him awake with a jerk, causing him to sit up - his pistol in his hand - the hammer cocked back.

The black stallion raised its head and nickered. Clay gave a nervous chuckle as he ran the fingers of his free hand through his thick mat of slightly graying hair. Tracking Curly Beeler was taking its toll.

"Alright, alright, I slept in a bit, don't make an issue about it," he yelled at the big stallion. "And, yes, I know we've got a big day ahead of us," he said as he rolled out of bed and slapped his hat on his head. Next, he shook a scorpion out of one of his boots before putting them on. This was a dangerous land and for a man to survive, he had to be careful of what might climb into his boots at night.

He was too keyed up to think about breakfast. Food was the last thing on his mind. Besides, there wasn't anything to cook until he replaced his supplies.

Clay covered the coals with dirt mixed with sand and poured the remains of cold coffee over any hot coals that might be left. The hunt was about to come to an end and he was anxious to finally have done with it.

The big horse seemed to know what was going on with his master and was as eager to get moving as Clay was. The big horse nickered again and pawed at the cold ground showing his desire to be on the way.

Clay Brentwood checked his pistol to make sure all of the cylinders were loaded. There would be no honor in what he was about to do and there was no use pretending there would be. When he had filled all the cylinders of the big forty-four-caliber pistol, Clay stepped into the saddle and pointed the black stallion in the direction of the small town.

As Clay rode down the mountainside, a calm settled over him - all his worries seemed to disappear. He was riding down to do a job that needed done and that was the long and the short of it. Nothing more needed saying or thinking about.

Clay and the black stallion entered the town limits of Bristol Springs, just as people were beginning to stir.

The black stallion, it's head held in regal splendor, danced down the dusty street less than two hours after the sun brought news of the coming day.

On his back, a stranger with a tied down widow maker on his hip rode easily in the saddle. Clay Brentwood looked neither left nor right, yet his eyes shaded by the brim of his hat, missed nothing. At this time of morning, only a few people were on the streets. Those that were, stopped and shaded their eyes and watched as the big horse and the stranger passed by.

One young woman in particular caught Clay's peripheral vision. She was about to enter a shop but stopped and turned slowly to look at him from beneath a flat brimmed Spanish style hat. Clay's heart skipped a beat. Their eyes locked for no more than the blink of an eyelid, and then she turned and hurried into the store, the hint of a smile on her lips.

Keeping his eyes looking straight ahead, Clay pulled the loop from over the hammer of his forty-four pistol, allowing him to pull the big hog-leg and do battle at the first sign of trouble none came – at least not right away.

Reining in at the sheriff's office, Clay ground hitched the big stallion, knowing the horse would stand quietly, waiting for his master to return.

Looking through the front window, the sheriff's office appeared to be empty.

"Where can I find the sheriff?" Clay asked of the elderly man who was sweeping the wooden porch in front of the sheriff's office.

An old man, with a bent back and watery eyes stopped his sweeping and stared up at Clay for a long moment. Leaning on his broom, he looked past Clay and admired the big stallion that stood without being snubbed to the hitch rail. That was some horse, he thought to himself, wondering how this stranger had come to be riding such a fine-looking piece of horseflesh - him dressed like a man who couldn't afford to own such an animal. After a moment, his eyes drifted back to Clay and the pistol hanging on Clay's hip. When he saw no badge on Clay's shirt, he asked, "You the law?"

"No sir, just a man passin' through," Clay said. "But I might have some business with the law here in town if he happens to be somewhere nearby."

Pointing toward the office, Clay continued. "Looks to me like the sheriff's office is empty, and I thought you might be the kind ah man who keeps his eyes open, and just could be, know where he is," Clay said through a wide grin.

On the ride into town, Clay had decided to check out the local law before making his final decision.

The old man eyed the stranger, and then spit a stream of tobacco juice into the dusty street. "Down at the cemetery. You can find the sheriff down at the cemetery," the old man said. "The Beeler gang shot him four days ago when they treed this here town. So's, I reckon Curly Beeler is the law here now. Kinda self-appointed, ya might say. If'n you want ta talk to him, he's over to the cantina."

Clay touched a finger to the brim of his hat, "Much obliged old timer," he said as he turned and walked back toward the black stallion.

"Better shuck thet wider-maker, mister. Curly Beeler don't allow nobody ta pack a weapon in this town ceptin' him and his gang," the old man called toward Clay's back.

The hint of a smile appeared on Clay's lips as he stepped into the saddle and turned the black stallion toward the livery stable down at the far end of the street.

Clay felt bad about the sheriff but the truth was, this made his decision easier. With no law around to interfere, he was free to do what needed to be done. In a sense, he would be acting as the law, judge and jury, along with bein' the one to carry out their death sentences.

As he rode up to the livery barn and stepped down, he glanced down the street and saw the old man hot-footing it toward the cantina. Curly would soon hear about the stranger who had just ridden into town, packin' hardware.

Clay saw no one to turn his horse over to so he stripped the stallion of his saddle and halter, then gave him a quick rubdown with a piece of gunnysack he found hanging over the railing of the stall. The horse nickered and shook his head as he was turned into a stall and given a small bucket of oats and a pitchfork of hay.

Emerging from the barn, Clay was confronted by two hard looking men who were standing in the middle of the street. Curly had wasted no time.

The one on Clay's left was tall and rangy, dressed in a black suit. He wore a white shirt with a string tie that had silver tips at each end. The gunman had a turned down mouth that sported a pencil thin mustache and eyes as cold as winter rain; a brace of pistols tied down in the gunfighter's style was all the warning Clay needed.

The other man was shorter and built more like an oak tree stump. His eyes were bloodshot and his teeth were yellow-brown. The stub of an unlit cigar was clamped tightly in his teeth. His clothes were worn and wrinkled. Clay would bet the man didn't shave or bathe on a regular basis. Instead of a sidearm, he carried a sawed off double barrel shotgun, called, a stagecoach gun. Both hammers were thumbed back.

The man dressed like a gunfighter was trying to take the stranger's measure and was puzzled. The stranger was not a tall man, maybe five foot eight but looked lean and well-muscled. He would guess the man to weigh around a hundred and sixty or seventy pounds; it was hard to tell. But the man definitely didn't fit the image of a gunfighter. His Levis were worn and patched, his boots were old and scuffed – and his once dark blue shirt had seen too many hard days in the sun.

Upon further inspection, the gunfighter found his answer under the wide brimmed hat that shaded the stranger's eyes.

Even though the stranger's eyes showed no hint of fear, or anger, or emotion of any kind, those eyes told the gunfighter somebody was about to die, and for the first time in his life, he felt a shiver run down his spine.

"Ain't nobody allowed ta carry ah gun, ceptin' us," the man with the shotgun said. "So, jest unbuckle yer holster and let'er drop."

Beyond the two men in front of him, Clay Brentwood saw faces peeking around corners and from behind closed curtains.

High up to his left, a man stood on the roof of the saloon holding a rifle loosely in his hand while he puffed on a cigarette. The man looked to be nothing more than your everyday loser who hired his gun out instead of working at an honest job. The man seemed none too concerned about whether the two gunmen in the street could handle one lone drifter, so he just stood there, casual like, waiting for the show to be over.

With a slight movement of his eyes, Clay checked the sun. It was on his right and their left, giving neither of them any advantage.

When the roar of gunfire subsided and the smoke disappeared, except for three dead men, the street was empty. No one had seen the stranger draw; nor did they see him dive to his right as his colt delivered three deadly pieces of lead. And no one saw him come to his feet and sprint down the alley. The dance was over before anyone realized it had begun.

Blue-gray gun smoke drifted into the cloudless sky as the sun beat down on the three dead men who were already beginning to draw flies.

When the gun smoke disappeared, people came out to take a closer look at the three dead men. Each and every one of the townspeople who had witnessed this event, secretly smiled beneath their sombreros and bonnets as they turned away and went about their business.

Curly took a long pull at the bottle of tequila and tried to fit everything together in his mind. He licked salt off the back of his hand and then sucked on a piece of lime. Three of his best men were lying dead in the street, and no one had a clue as to the identity of the man who did it. This total stranger had walked out of the barn and without saying a word, shot three of his men and then disappeared like a whiff of smoke.

Curly took another pull from the bottle, his mind in a whirl. "This man has to be a Texas Ranger," he said to the other men in the saloon. "No one else would have the brass to stand against me like that."

Curly's hand was shaking as he reached once more for the bottle and its nerve calming liquid. After his third drink, his nerves were beginning to calm down some when one of his men charged in through the bat-winged doors and headed straight to the bar. The man called Leroy was young, in his twenties, and had a pug face that made him look like he'd been smashed in the face with the underside of a frying pan.

"You ain't gonna believe this boss," the shaggy headed gunslinger spit out. "That feller yer ah lookin' fer is down at the restaurant, sittin' there, calm as a mill pond, eatin' his breakfast."

"You sure it's him?" Curly asked.

"Seen him with my own eyes!" the young man said. "I was in there havin' a cup of coffee when he come ah walkin' in like he didn't have ah care in the world, sat down at ah table and ordered his breakfast."

"And you didn't do anything?" Curly asked.

"Sure, I did. I come down here ta tell you."

After a moment, his eyes grew wide. "You didn't think I was gonna try and take him all by myself, did ya? After what he did ta Blackie and Stump and Tom?"

"No, I reckon not," Curly said, shaking his head. "You ain't got the cajones."

The young gunslinger frowned and ordered a beer, gulped it down, then went over to a table and sat down across from another young gunslinger about his own age who was playing solitaire with a deck of worn out cards.

Curly made a motion with his hand and four sour faced gunmen left their table and walked over to the bar.

"You boys go down to that restaurant and tell that fella I want to talk to him and then escort him back here."

"Well. . . supposin' he don't wanna come?" one of them asked.

"Then kill him!" Curly said with a snarl.

The four gun hands looked at each other, and as one, headed for the front door.

From where Clay sat, he could see the street and watched as the four gun slicks nervously came down the street, talking back and forth as though they were discussing a plan of attack.

After taking another bite of ham and eggs, Clay took a long sip from his coffee cup, then stood up and made his way to a darkened corner. "Just stay in the kitchen and hunker down behind something," Clay said to the man behind the counter. "I'm guessin' there's ah bit more dancin' ta be done."

Clay reached a dark corner and turned around, his right hand hovering above the colt hanging on his hip as the four gun slicks entered the restaurant with pistols already clutched in their fists.

"You lookin' for me?" he asked.

As one, the four men spun in his direction, raising their pistols as they did so; but before even one pistol discharged its lethal ball of lead, Clay's big colt belched out four death warrants so fast it almost sounded like one long, loud, roar.

The restaurant owner would later say the stranger walked over to his table, sat down and finished his breakfast in a leisurely fashion, then stood up and ambled out the back door like nothing had happened. The dollar tip the stranger left on the table was never mentioned.

Along with the rest of the town, Curly heard the gunfire and assumed his hired guns had killed the stranger. For the first time today, he began to relax. It was over. If the man had some identification papers on him, he would find out who this stranger was. Not that it mattered all that much, especially now. The man was dead and the town was his again. Curly poured himself another shot of tequila.

Many of the townsfolk were saddened by the thought that the stranger could be dead. They were just getting used to the idea that he might be the one to kill Curly and his gang, or at least run them out of town.

When the owner of the restaurant came down the street, informing everyone he met about what had happened, they quietly but discreetly cheered the stranger on.

The restaurant owner hurried on to the cantina to tell Curly what had happened in the hopes that Curly would go easy on him for bringing the news that his gun hands were dead. He knew it would go harder on him if he said nothing.

The restaurant owner stood in front of Curly and recited what had taken place, wringing his hands on his apron, hoping and praying Curly wouldn't shoot him. Curly was known to be a man of moods.

When the restaurant owner finished his story, a cold chill ran through Curly like someone had dumped a bucket of ice water on him. Curly waved the restaurant owner away, turned to the bar and reached for the half empty bottle of tequila. Who the hell was this man? Curly began to shake at the thought of the man coming for him next. He took a long pull at the tequila bottle and sighed as the liquid burned deep down inside him.

Curly had only two men left and he motioned to them. They reluctantly stood up and made their way in his direction, neither one wanting to brace the stranger even more afraid of Curly.

Curly checked his pistol to make sure it was loaded with six rounds. He wanted to load this stranger up with as much lead as he could.

Curly and his last two pistoleros stood, guns in their fists, facing the bat-wing front doors. "We don't talk, we just shoot as soon as he comes through those doors," Curly said with an edge of fear in his voice.

Even though they had been standing there less than two minutes, it seemed like an eternity and their pistols felt like huge weights in their hands. Each one of them was close to his breaking point when a voice behind them spoke only one word, "Beeler!"

Curly and his two remaining gun hands spun around, unloading their pistols in the direction of the voice, their bullets killing the back wall.

A few feet to the right, Clay's pistol exploded three times. The remaining two would-be outlaws were kicked backward - bullet holes in their chests. They were dead by the time they hit floor.

Curly felt the pain as a bullet plowed its way through his right shoulder. Unable to control his fingers, his pistol slipped from his hand and landed on the floor. Curly looked down and saw blood gushing from his wound - staining his white shirt.

"Who the hell are you? I got ah right ta know!" Curly shouted; fear seeping out of him as thick as honey dripping from a comb.

Clay stood there, taking his time, while he reloaded his pistol, watching and waiting to see if there were any more of Curly's men to deal with. Counting in his head, he believed Curly was the only one left, and when no one else showed up, Clay eased the big colt back into its place in the well-worn holster, and then walked over and stood close to the infamous outlaw.

While Curly stood in front of him, bleeding and shaking, Clay rolled a cigarette and lit it, drawing deeply of the smoke, and then blowing it into Curly's face, "Two and a half years ago you put a rifle bullet along the side of my head and thought you'd killed me. I was stunned and couldn't move I wasn't dead. As a matter of fact, I watched as you and your gang raped and murdered my wife, which also killed our unborn child. And you and your men laughed the whole time. Next, you burned my house and barn and stole my horses along with what few cattle I had in the corrals."

Clay took another puff from the cigarette and blew the smoke into the air, slowly. “It took me awhile ta get back on my feet I did, and I’ve been just two steps behind you ever since,” he said, staring into Curly’s eyes, hoping of seeing some semblance of him remembering the incident even with the information he’d given Curly, Curly’s eyes were still blank. It was as though the whole affair had no meaning for him, which made Clay even angrier. How could he do such violent things and not even remember it? Things like rape and murder and stealin’ meant so little to Curly that he didn’t bother with remembering the suffering and grief he left in his wake.

Taking his time, Clay smoked his cigarette while he tried to let his anger subside time did little to relieve his pain. Curly just stood there staring back at him with a blank stare, wondering what the stranger was going to do next?

Clay wanted to smash Curly’s face in with his fists; beat him until he was dead instead, he took a deep breath, trying to will himself to remain calm, which didn’t work, his desire for revenge was strong. After a moment, he reached out and shoved the lit end of his cigarette into Curly’s bloody wound.

Curly let out a scream and tried to remove the burning cigarette Clay stayed his hand and watched Curly suffer until he passed out.

Clay grabbed the bottle of tequila from the bar and poured it into Curly’s face and waited. When Curly opened his eyes, Clay dragged him to his feet and slapped his face. Next, he pulled a long, double-edged knife from its sheath and held it in front of Curly’s bulging eyes. “This little pig sticker is called an Arkansas Toothpick and its razor sharp on both sides. Can you guess what’s gonna happen next?”

Curly's breath was now coming in ragged bursts and little noises came from somewhere deep inside his throat. He wanted to break loose and run the stranger held him in a tight grip and his right arm was useless.

"My wife used to read a lot from the good book at night after supper. I remember part of one of the passages that seems ta fit this occasion," Clay said. "An eye for an eye and a tooth for a tooth." He smiled at the suffering he could see in Curly's eyes. "And that's what I've been doin' here today, Curly, collectin' what the good book says I'm entitled to collect," Clay said.

Curly tried to talk nothing came out. A wet spot began to form on the front of his pants and his breathing became even more ragged. He was going to die at the hands of this man and there wasn't a damn thing he could do about it.

Clay looked Curly in the eyes and saw a dead man standing in front of him. "You ain't nothin' but ah cowardly piece of scum that doesn't deserve ta breathe the same air as decent folks. Without somebody backin' you up, you're just another two-bit killer that ain't worth the price of ah bullet," Clay said as he reached out and sliced Curly's throat from ear to ear, then tossed him to the floor.

Staring down at the dying outlaw, Clay's insides were filled with rage. He wanted Curly to know what it meant to suffer before he drew his last breath.

After a long moment, when the anger inside him began to subside, Clay came to his senses and his hands began to tremble. The rage he'd felt ever since the loss of his beloved wife and their unborn child was beginning to subside. Two and a half years of pent up anger had been lifted from his shoulders. It was finally over.

Clay wiped his knife on Curly's shirtsleeve, and then tossed a twenty-dollar gold-piece toward the barman, who caught it easily. "This should take care of what needs cleanin' up, plus you can keep whatever you find in their pockets along with their horses and gear."

With eyes wide, the bartender whispered, "Yes sir."

The bartender watched as the famous Curly Beeler, head of the most notorious gang in that part of the country, lay on the floor of his cantina - blood spewing from his neck as he gagged out his death song. He would leave the bloodstain on the floor. He would cordon it off. It would mean a lot of money. Men would come from miles around to see the spot and hear the story. The stranger had done him a big favor today.

Clay Brentwood walked through the bat-wing doors and drew in a large breath of fresh air, then blew it out slowly, trying to come to terms with what he'd just done. He was not a man killer in this case, revenge was needed, and he'd obliged.

By the time the bat-wings had finished swinging back and forth, Curly Beeler was no longer among the living and his rotten soul was headed straight for hell.

At least that's where Clay hoped it would go as he sauntered causally down the street in the direction of the livery barn. People who had been gathered outside the saloon parted to let him pass, afraid to say anything.

As soon as he entered the barn, the men of the town rushed inside the cantina.

After gawking at Curly's body and the pool of blood, they bellied up to the bar where the bartender was passing out whiskey as fast as he could pour, all the while, telling them everything he'd seen and heard, with the restaurant owner tossing in his two cents worth, when he could get a word in.

Standing at the door, several of the townswomen, including the young woman wearing a Spanish style hat, were committing to memory every word the bartender and restaurant owner was saying. They would repeat the story many times over.

"We ought ta give that fella ah reward," one of the men at the bar said.

The men all shook their heads in agreement not one of them offered to go down to the barn.

Fifteen minutes later, the people watched as the black stallion pranced down the center of the street with the stranger riding easily on his back.

Some were happy to see him go. A man who could shoot down ten men and not blink an eye was not the kind of man they wanted ruling the roost over their town. On the other hand, if this man wanted to take over the job of sheriff, they could all rest more peacefully at night.

Still, no one hailed him to ask him to stay and keep the peace in their quiet little town. As far as they were concerned, he was just the stranger who rode into town on a black stallion, killed Curly Beeler and his gang, then rode away without a word, as though this was something he did on a regular basis.

Though no one knew his name, or where he came from, the story of his short visit would become that of legend, and the blood on the floor of the cantina would be proof that Curly Beeler had died here.

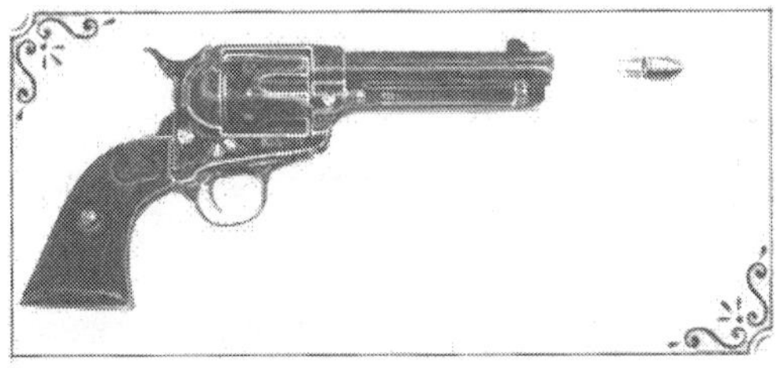

CHAPTER THREE

-

At the edge of town, the horse took the road heading south as if it was his idea, then stretched his legs into a comfortable lope; the familiar weight on his back and the rider allowing him the freedom to do as he pleased.

The big horse seemed to remember his days of freedom; racing through the hills and valleys with his herd of mares chasing after him until the day he stepped on a rock and twisted his leg. His leg had swelled up so bad he couldn't walk. As he lay on the ground, waiting to die, this man had come along and somehow got him on his feet and took him home with him and hung him in a contraption until his leg had healed.

The man was good to him and fed him and rubbed his sore leg with something that made his nose burn. The man rubbed his neck and back and fed him apples. When he was well, the man released him to go back to his mares and his old way of life for reasons he didn't understand, he didn't run away. This man-beast had saved his life and fed him and treated him with kindness. The man-beast was now his master and he would stay with him as long as the man-beast needed him.

Clay Brentwood was in deep thought and paid little attention to where they were going as long as the big stallion stayed on the road. Clay had no real destination. He was trying to calm down from the killing spree he'd unleashed.

Each day for nearly two and a half years, with hate festering inside him, hate that begged for revenge, Clay had practiced with the colt, slowly gaining speed and accuracy. Before Curly's raid on his ranch, he had never fired a pistol in his life, and a rifle only for hunting meat. With a rifle, he was a crack shot, and now, after two and a half years of practicing, he was even better with a pistol.

Reflecting back, Clay realized that from the day he began the hunt until today, the big pistol on his hip and the horse between his legs, had been his only companions.

And now at last, the hunt was finally over. His wife and their unborn child had been avenged. "It's finally over, Martha. You can rest in peace, now," Clay whispered to the open sky.

For the first time in thirty long months, he had no idea what he would be doing tomorrow.

A shiver went through him as the realization of what he'd done today attached itself to his brain. Before today, he had never taken a human life;

yet less than an hour ago, he had taken the lives of ten men without giving them a second thought.

As he rode along, he wondered if the past two and a half years had turned him from a peace-loving rancher, into a bloodthirsty man killer?

And what did the future hold for him now that the hunt was over? Would he be able to hang up the big forty-four and go back to being a rancher? Or would what he'd done today, follow him wherever he went? He'd heard stories about other fast guns. Would young bucks that thought themselves a fast gun want ta challenge him in every town from here to the coast? Is that what he had to look forward to for the rest of his life? Maybe he should change his name and deny ever being in this part of the country.

By now, the sun had reached the middle of the sky and waves of heat danced across the desert floor like Arabian belly dancers. A roadrunner raced across the hot sand as though he couldn't allow his feet to stay in one spot too long for fear of burning his feet.

Clay rolled and lit a cigarette, blowing smoke into the hot afternoon, trying to get his mind focused. The one thing he kept telling himself over and over was, he was no killer and wanted no more of this kind of life.

Sure, over the past two and a half years he'd gotten very fast on the draw, and he could shoot the whiskers off a fly that was because of the constant practicing and the hatred gnawing at his insides.

During that time, he would practice as he rode down this or that trail by seeing how fast he could draw and put a bullet into a tree or piece of cactus. Sometimes he would shoot live prey to provide a moving target and meat for his supper. Day by day he saw himself getting faster and more and more accurate until his draw and firing was done without thought. By now, he rarely missed what he aimed at. Looking back, he realized he had not consciously considered the fact that when he caught up with Curly and his gang, they would be shooting back.

Never far from his thoughts, was the fact that Curly Beeler and his gang had brutally raped and murdered his wife. How could they do that to a pregnant woman who was near her birthing time, he wondered; or any woman for that matter? Even though he'd tried to shut the sounds from his mind, he'd heard her screams, begging them to stop. But they hadn't. Instead they increased their violence by slapping and beating her. He'd heard everything and had been helpless to do anything. He'd tried to get up and find his rifle his limbs wouldn't move, he was paralyzed. Nor could he speak, to beg them to stop. Though his eyes were swollen almost shut, he could still see through the thin slits. The faces of Curly and the ruthless men who rode with him were inscribed on his brain like a tintype photograph. It was because of the pain in his heart that made him practice every day, not caring whether they shot back or didn't. They would die and that would be the end of it. Whether he was also killed, didn't matter, not as long as they were all dead first.

If his neighbor, Marion Sooner and his wife Rebecca hadn't come along a few hours after Curly and his gang left, he wasn't sure he would have survived the hungry coyotes that were closing in on him for an easy kill, and a full belly. That part of Texas was overrun with coyotes to the point the state had a bounty on them. Marion Sooner had pulled his wagon to a stop, picked up his rifle, and made nine easy dollars that day.

For two weeks, Rebecca had doctored Clay as he lay in a semi-coma, thrashing about in a delirium, seeing the scene over and over in his mind.

Marion had gone back over to Clay's ranch and searched through the ashes left from the fire and gathered up what he could find of Martha's remains, and after carefully wrapping them in a piece of canvas, he buried them under the big oak tree at the edge of the yard. With a piece of board, he scratched her name on it and stuck it at the head of the grave.

For a week after he'd come out of his coma, Clay suffered in grief, wishing he had died along with his wife. She had been his rock, and with the baby coming they had made plans. Each day he slipped deeper and deeper into his depression until one day Marion asked him to go for a walk with him. "We need to talk," he'd told Clay.

By the end of their walk, anger had taken over the grief and he vowed to get his strength back and find the men that had taken his life away from him.

Two days later, Clay borrowed a horse from Marion and rode over to what was left of his place, and there under the big oak tree, he vowed to Martha to bring down his wrath on Curly and his gang for what they had done. He found another piece of wood and carved her name, date of birth, date of death and the words, 'Died before her time.'

After leaving her grave, he'd ridden into town and purchased a Colt six-shooter pistol, a fast draw holster and six boxes of ammunition, along with a new lever action rifle, in case he needed to do some long-range shooting. The following morning, out behind Marion Sooner's barn, Clay Brentwood began learning to fast draw his pistol and hit what he pointed it at. From the start, he hit almost everything he aimed at. He was a natural still felt he could do better.

A few days later, while he was out riding to get his strength back, he saw a horse lying on its side. It was alive barely. He must have been there for some time with no food or water. The right front leg was badly injured. Clay carefully checked the leg and found it wasn't broken, only badly bruised and swollen.

When he stood up, he took a good look at the horse and let out a long whistle. The big stallion was black as coal and looked to be at least sixteen hands - probably the leader of the herd of wild horses that roamed this part of the country. More than likely this was the same horse that had come onto the ranch to try and steal his mares.

Clay inspected the big horse, finding several scars to prove his leadership.

It took Clay better than an hour to get the horse up and standing. He had no food but poured water from his canteen into his hat and let the horse drink, helping him regain at least a fraction of his strength. Then another three hours to get him back to the ranch where he could doctor him. It was slow going because the big horse was weak and had to hobble on three legs. Clay let him take his time, plus it took a bit for the wild horse to get used to the lead rope around his neck.

With Marion's help, they rigged up a sling that fit under the horse's stomach and hung the black stallion in it to take pressure off the leg. At first, the black stallion didn't like having his feet off the ground with some hand feeding and soft talking, the big horse settled down.

Over the next few weeks, Clay doctored the black stallion until his leg was well. Leading him outside the barn, he released him to return to wherever he came from instead of running away, the black stallion put his nose against Clay's chest and nuzzled him. From that day on, they were inseparable. The horse seemed to sense Clay's grief and found ways to take Clay's mind off of his worries - like coming up behind him and nudging him with his nose, then laying his chin over his new master's shoulder, or nipping him lightly on the shoulder. Clay would grin and take a treat of some kind from his pocket and reward the big horse for his friendship.

Marion and his wife made several comments about how it was the best horse - man relationship they'd ever seen. Marion commented to his wife several times that the horse seemed to know what Clay wanted him to do before Clay, himself, did.

At the dinner table the night before leaving on his quest, Clay told Marion and his wife that a few months after he and Martha were married, she informed him that her father, as a wedding gift, had paid off their mortgage, so the ranch was theirs free and clear. When Clay queried her, she confessed that she came from money, which surprised Clay. He knew she was educated she had never mentioned being rich. She was a down to earth kind of woman and loved being a rancher's wife.

As it turned out, her father owned several lucrative businesses in and around Wichita, Kansas, including a bank and several thousand acres of land. She went on to explain that her name was on all the titles and business deals, so that if anything should happen to her father there would be no hassles with her taking over, which would make them the richest ranchers in that part of the country.

A few weeks later, an attorney from Wichita showed up with papers for Clay to sign, and when Clay asked what he was signing, the attorney informed him that his name had been added to all the properties and businesses.

Martha had smiled and told him it was her birthday gift to him, plus, Martha was excited about the baby and informed Clay it would definitely be a boy who would one day inherit everything.

Clay didn't understand how she could know such things he was happy about the thought of becoming a father. The ranch was coming along nicely. They would sit on the porch at night and he would play his guitar while she sang. Clay could not imagine how he'd gotten so lucky.

Then came the day they received word that her father had died of a heart attack. Clay asked Marion to watch over the place while they were gone to the funeral.

Since there were no trains near their ranch, they took the buggy Clay had purchased for the trip up to Wichita. Taking a buggy that far worried Clay some because of all the jostling around Martha would be taking. She had smiled at his concern, and patted him on the cheek, assuring him she would be all right.

Practically everyone in Wichita turned out for the funeral. A large, black wagon pulled by four black horses carried her father to the cemetery where he was laid to rest.

They stood in line for over two hours receiving condolences and shaking people's hands. Clay never realized how many friends one man could have.

The following day, after a lot of paper signing, the attorney agreed, for a fee, to keep an eye on things for them.

Clay had wanted to spend a couple of extra days so Martha could rest and see the doctor as soon as the doctor told her she was fine, she wanted to go home.

The trip had gone smoothly and they had only been back two days before Curly and his men came riding in and turned his world upside down. If only he'd insisted they stay longer in Wichita.

The scraping of Rebecca's chair brought Clay back to the present. He stared at his plate, realizing he was about to embark on a mission that he would not give up on until his wife's death had been avenged.

While Rebecca was cleaning up the dishes, Clay wrote out a declaration on a piece of brown paper, giving Marion ownership of the bull he had loaned him, prior to the raid, along with the right to use his land for whatever purpose he saw fit until sometime in the future when he, Clay Brentwood, might return. If, in five years he had not returned, the land and all its stock would become the sole property of Marion and Rebecca Sooner.

Marion protested, telling Clay that the ranch would always be his, no matter how long it took for him to get back. He and Rebecca made Clay swear to come back.

After agreeing, they shook hands and an agreement was struck between them. The only problem was - Clay wasn't sure he could ever live on that land again. There would be too many memories.

First, he had his promise to Martha to keep, and then he would see.

Two months after Curly Beeler and his gang had created a giant void in Clay's world, Clay left the Sooner's front yard, leading an extra horse loaded down with food, supplies and a lot of things he really didn't want or need was too polite to say no to. He figured he would find folks along the way who needed the extra things. Waves and shouts about being careful and hurrying back followed him far down the road.

Clay would never forget the Sooners' and what they'd done for him. He hoped he would live long enough to keep his promise and to return one day. When he did, maybe they could partner up. Marion was a good man with both horses and cattle, and he was honest. Clay knew he couldn't ask for a better partner for now he knew he couldn't go back - not yet. He needed time to get his head on straight and make sure he could handle the memories that he was sure would haunt him when he saw her grave again.

If he did return, maybe he could live in town or build a new house on a different part of the ranch, which to him didn't make sense, since originally, the house had been built on the best location anywhere on their land. She even had a well in the kitchen. And living in town meant a long ride twice a day, plus he wouldn't be able to watch over the place if trouble came again.

These were all things he would need to come to terms with after his search for Curly and his gang was over, if he was still alive, that is.

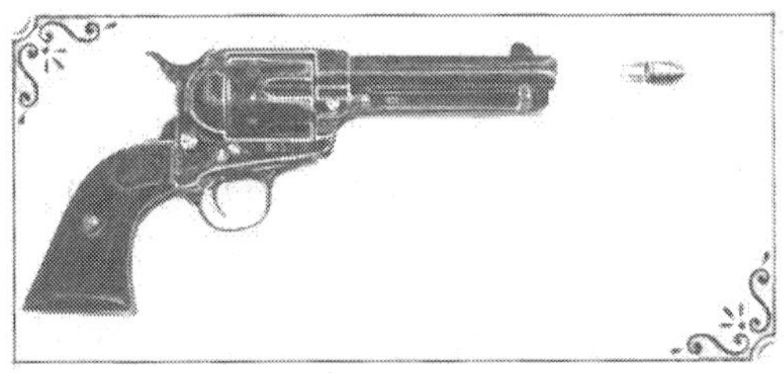

CHAPTER FOUR

-

The big stallion nickered and brought Clay back to the present. He looked around slowly saw no danger, just the blistering sun and the dusty road ahead of him.

In this part of the New Mexico Territory, the land was much the same as it had been millions of years ago – dry, desolate, and deadly to any man who did not know how to survive. Water was scarce and hard to find. It seemed to be mainly in places only known to the Indians who lived here and a very few white men.

He rode in silence letting his keyed-up nerves settle down. Today he had walked a thin line between justice and out and out murder. And now that it was over, instead of feeling like a murderer, he felt like he had done the world a service by eliminating Curly and his gang. The world would be a better place without men like them – at least that's the way he had to look at it to keep a sane mind. Besides, Clay figured the courts would have hung them hanged or shot, dead was dead, he reasoned.

Clay stopped the big horse long enough to roll and light another cigarette, then sat and stared at the sky while his horse munched on what little scrub grass there was to be had along the road.

Small clouds drifted lazily across the sky, moving to who knew where as Clay pondered his future. During the past two and a half years, he had lived for the most part, on the trail and had spent very little money, buying only the bare necessities. Before the raid on his ranch, he had approximately seven thousand dollars in the bank. He had a natural way with horses and they sold for a premium, and his reputation was growing.

After his recovery, he'd informed the attorney in Wichita about the raid on the ranch and Martha's death. The attorney replied back, giving Clay his condolences and told him not to worry; he would do all the necessary paperwork to put everything in Clay's name now that he was the sole survivor. In the letter, the attorney also included the name of the bank and the account number, should Clay need funds. The cash funds in the bank alone amounted to sixty-five thousand dollars, not counting what came in each day from the various businesses. Plus, there were several thousand acres of ranch or farmland property, should Clay want to sell.

A quick calculation in Clay's head came to the tidy sum of seventy-one thousand dollars cash on hand the day he left in pursuit of Curly.

As best as he could figure, during the thirty months he'd been on the road, he had spent somewhere in the neighborhood of eight hundred dollars, leaving him over seventy thousand dollars to restart his life with, plus whatever the amount had grown to by now. By his way of thinking, he was a rich man. And he had friends, along with a fine piece of property of his own to go back to in Texas - if that's what he decided to do.

As much as he loved the land, he wasn't sure he was ready. Martha had loved the ranch; it was her home. If he went back now, he would be forced to see her grave each and every day and he didn't know how he would handle all the memories it would bring up. She had been his life.

Maybe he'd go back just long enough to give the property to Marion and his wife. He knew they would tend to Martha's grave and keep it free of weeds and such.

He could go out to California and buy some land or possibly a business. Or he might go up north to Montana. He'd heard there were large herds of wild horses up there that were free for the catching. He wondered if there might be horses like his black stallion up there? He knew of men from back east who would pay a pretty penny for a horse like the one he was riding. As far as another woman in his life - he knew Martha would not want him to live alone, nor did he want to he would just let that happen when, and if, it was supposed to. In the meantime, he would concentrate on getting rid of his gunfighter image.

By now, the cigarette was down to just a nub and he crushed what was left between his thumb and first finger; then spread the tobacco and shreds of paper to the wind.

Without being told, the big horse lifted his head and started down the road again at a leisurely lope.

Rounding a curve in the road, Clay saw a buggy with its rear wheels off in the ditch and a woman standing with her back to him.

As he rode up, the woman turned to face him. Clay's chest constricted and his throat went dry. Standing in front of him was the most beautiful woman he'd ever laid eyes on, and that took some doing because until now, Martha was the most beautiful woman he'd ever seen.

This woman had raven black hair that hung loosely down to the middle of her back and she was dressed in the style of Spanish aristocracy. She had an exquisite figure and in her eyes he saw nobility and strength, yet her skin looked to be as soft as doeskin.

Then it hit him like a bolt of lightning. This was the woman he'd seen standing in the doorway of the shop when he'd ridden into town this very morning!

Without a word, Clay stepped from the saddle and walked over to the buggy and grabbed the back of it in his hands. Calling out to the horse, he lifted the buggy and shoved. The horse leaned into the harness and easily pulled the wagon back onto the road, then stopped when Clay yelled, "Whoa."

The young woman stood by quietly, her hands clasped in front of her, apprising this man she had seen only once for some reason, was strangely attracted to.

After the shooting, she heard the story from the barman about the man's wife and unborn child he would never know. Something clutched at her heart and she had raced her buggy by an alternate route and purposely put the rear wheels of the buggy in the ditch, hoping to get his attention. She wanted to look deep into the eyes of a man who would do battle with ten bloodthirsty killers because of his love for a woman.

As the man turned and walked in her direction, their eyes met and once again something inside of her stirred. She knew this man was not a ruthless killer a man of strength and honor; a man who had quietly ridden into town, did what needed to be done, and then ridden away. This was a man she wanted to know more about.

Without waiting for him to introduce himself, she stepped up and said, "Senor', my name is Victoria Marie Christina Claire Ontiveros. I am the owner of a very large ranchero not far from here. My late husband and many of our loyal, hardworking charros, men you call cowboys, were killed by that Curly Beeler and his bunch of miscreants. Between them and the Comancheros, many horses and cattle have been stolen. It has been hard for me, and I confess to you that I am at my wits end trying to run the ranchero all by myself. I am in desperate need of a Segundo; a foreman, as you call them. And from what I have seen and heard today, I believe you are the man to handle the job. If you are looking for work, I would appreciate it very much if you would come work for me."

Now, just inches apart, she looked directly into his eyes and licked her lips. "I believe you would find me most generous."

Clay wasn't sure why he made the decision he did. Maybe it was because of something he'd read in a book by one of those English writers, where a shining knight comes to the aid of a fair maiden, or something along those lines.

After a long pause, Clay smiled and said, "What should I call you, boss, ma'am, or Senora?"

They walked together to the buggy where Clay took her arm and assisted her up, then climbed up and sat down next to her. After taking up the reins and giving the horse a light tap on its hindquarters, he gave a whistle and the black stallion fell in behind the buggy.

Victoria Marie Christina Claire Ontiveros smiled and said, "Victoria. You may call me Victoria when we are alone and Senora when we are not. And what should I call you, Senor'?"

"Clay Brentwood is my name you can just call me, Clay. Now then, about my duties?"

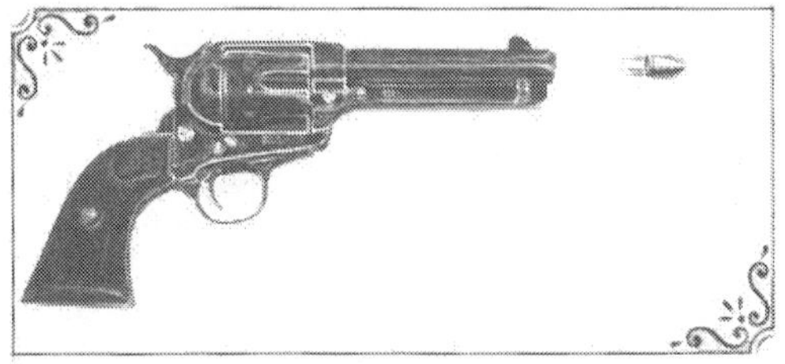

CHAPTER FIVE

-

The trip to her ranchero would take close to half a day and for the first time in many a moon Clay Brentwood was at peace with himself. As they traveled down the dusty road, they talked about his duties and her plans for the ranchero, which Clay liked. This woman was not only beautiful had a head on her shoulders as well. Clay made a mental note of the land as they went along while his new boss told him about Spanish land grants and such. A man never had too much information, so he listened and stored it away.

What caught his attention most was when she told him her marriage had been an arranged affair between her father and her late husband, Santiago Ontiveros, who was more than thirty years older than she was.

He'd heard about such things but had never actually been acquainted with anyone who was a party of such an arrangement.

"We had been married only seven months before Senor' Beeler shot him. My husband and a few of our charros tried to stop Senor' Beeler and his gang from stealing our cattle and horses when the fight was over, Senor' Beeler left one of our charros alive to bring my husband and the others back, face down across their horses - along with a warning to stay out of his way or the next time he would burn us out.

"Before that, the Comancheros had already stolen many horses and cattle and killed several of our charros. For me, this was the last straw. A lone woman cannot run such a place as this without a strong Segundo," she said, waving her arms from side to side, "And since I did not have a strong Segundo, I have been considering selling the ranchero. But I have not done so for two reasons. First, even though I was never in love with my husband, I have fallen in love with this land and the ranchero and I do not want to leave it. Until now, I have never truly owned anything in my entire life," she said. "Secondly, I cannot abide giving all of this up without a fight."

Clay found himself admiring this courageous young woman who could be living in the lap of luxury in any city she chose instead, chose to live out in the middle of nowhere on a piece of land that fought you tooth and nail for existence.

As it turned out, the ranchero covered a little over fifty square miles. A ranch this size amounted to more acres than his mind could wrap around at the moment.

"A good deal of it is desert there are hidden valleys where water and grass grows to knee high, if you know where to find them. They are ideal places to raise both horses and cattle, and I'm sure there are valleys we haven't found yet," she said, giving him a look that let him know he would need to be in the saddle a lot.

She sighed and wiped her forehead with a handkerchief, then continued. "The land spreads out for miles from the hacienda, which allows the banditos to raid without anyone knowing about it for days. My last Segundo was in league with a group of Comancheros and was helping himself to our cattle before Curly and his bunch killed him.

"Ramon, the man who replaced him, is a good man and loyal to a fault he is not a strong leader. He is still young and has much to learn. Without the help of a strong Segundo who knows about horses and cattle, there is no way I can run this ranch all by myself."

Giving him a smile that would melt ice, she said, "Thank you for accepting the position. But I must warn you, it won't be easy."

"Well now ma'am, I. . ."

The glint of metal twinkled off to his left, just at the top of a small rise. Clamping his jaw shut, he slapped the reins down on the horse's hindquarters and felt the buggy lurch forward just as a bullet struck the bed right behind where Clay was sitting.

Clay grabbed his rifle and the Senora, then leaped into the ditch. At the same time, he allowed his eyes to scan the spot where the shot had come from like he'd been taught by, Sits a Horse. Sits a Horse was a

Comanche Indian who had worked for him, back in Texas, and had taught him much.

"Never look for a man or a horse or a buffalo on the horizon. Look at the land in a general broad view, seeing everything like a large picture; then allow your eyes to see anything that moves or doesn't belong. That is the Indian way of seeing things," Sits a Horse had said while scouting for strays.

So, with that in mind, Clay let his eyes roam the nearby hills just to the rear of them and saw something protruding over a boulder that looked out of place, like a rifle barrel propped on a rock. Slowly, he brought the Winchester to his shoulder and took notice of the height and distance, then squeezed the trigger. Clay felt the jar against his shoulder and heard the boom; then watched as rock splintered the exact spot where the rifle barrel was protruding over the boulder.

A loud scream filled the air and the rifle barrel disappeared followed by the sound of a horse running away.

Clay stood up and helped his new boss to her feet. "You wait right here. I'll go get the horse and buggy and come back to get you," Clay said as he started up out of the ditch.

"Oh no you won't!" Victoria shouted, "Not when men with guns are shooting at us. Plus, there are rattlesnakes out here! And I hate snakes! I'm going with you!"

Clay grinned as she grabbed a hold of his arm and they headed off down the road in pursuit of the wagon and runaway horse. They hadn't gone far when they saw the big stallion come trotting down the road in their direction.

When the big horse hauled up in front of them, he shook his head and nickered as if to say, "Well, climb aboard."

Clay was grinning from ear to ear as he stepped into the saddle, and then helped the Senora up behind him. When he felt her arms go around his waist and she pushed her body against his back, be blew out a long breath of air to calm his reaction, then nudged the big horse forward. Her being so close to him was more than just a little bit distracting, it was downright painful.

When they caught up to the buggy, Clay was more than glad to let the Senora drive the wagon, by herself.

Victoria smiled as she climbed onto the buggy seat. While she might be young and not a woman of the world, she was not stupid. As she lifted the reins and let them tap the mare on her hindquarters, her face felt flush and her breathing was more than a bit irregular. She too had felt the effects of being so close and having her arms around this strong man who had suddenly come into her life.

Clay was glad he was not sitting on the buggy seat next to Victoria. He wasn't sure he was up to the feelings that had taken possession of him when she had been so close. The feel of her arms around him, with her body pressing against his back and the smell of her, was nerve wracking. It had been a long time since he'd felt this way. He missed the nearness and companionship of his wife and he didn't want to be disloyal to Martha it was coming up on the close side of three years since he'd lost her, and to have these feelings, all of a sudden like, was very confusing.

Clay shook his head to clear his mind as he rode up next to the buggy. "Are you alright?" he asked.

She smiled and said, “If I had any doubts about you being my Segundo, that has been cleared up. Thank you for saving my life.”

“Have any idea who the shooter might be?” Clay asked, trying to change the subject.

“Since the Beeler gang is no longer around, I can only venture a guess. Maybe it was one of the Comancheros? I don’t know.”

Clay nodded. “How much further to your ranch?”

“We have been on my ranch for several hours now the hacienda is still beyond that mesa up ahead,” she answered pointing toward a flat top mesa to the southwest. As close as he could figure, the mesa was still a little more than a mile away across open country.

Clay glanced over his shoulder, scanning their back trail and the landscape on either side to make sure no one was following them. For the most part, the land was desert, with rolling hills and large mesas off to both sides. He knew he had a lot to learn about this country. He needed to know where the good valleys were, along with water holes that only the animals and Indians knew about. If a man was going to survive this barren land that looked the same as it did thousands of years ago, he would need to know what the Indians and Mexicans knew. When he felt sure they were alone, he turned his head back and rode along in silence, his eyes moving from side to side.

A short while later, as they rode along in the lea of the mesa, Clay looked up and felt small. The mesa was nearly three quarters of a mile long, a quarter of a mile wide and he guessed, close to six hundred feet high.

On the far side, the land dipped down into a large, fertile valley. The hacienda was a large, sprawling affair made of adobe brick, surrounded by a solid wall – similar to a fort, only nicer. A barn and five other smaller buildings sat inside the walls and in the vicinity of the big house. Attached to the barn, were several corrals where horses milled about. A large adobe brick wall surrounded the entire complex and he could see riders coming and going through the front gate. He could see slits near the tops of the walls that could be used for shooting, should someone attack. The man who built this must have had a military background.

As they descended into the valley, Clay did a quick count and came up with more than six hundred head of longhorn cattle grazing nearby.

As if anticipating his question, Victoria said, "This is only part of what we used to have. There is another herd, a little bigger than this one, in a valley beyond that mesa far to the west," she said, pointing toward the glaring sun. "And to you, that may seem to be a lot before the Comancheros and Curly Beeler came, we had several thousand head of cattle and close to three hundred horses. I hope to be moving this herd to a valley with good grass and water, soon.

Clay let out a whistle. This was what he was hoping to do with his spread back in Texas – before Curly and his bunch showed up. Except, he was planning on introducing some Hereford stock into the herd. In fact, he'd purchased a bull out of Kansas City not long before Curly showed up. Fortunately, he'd loaned him to Marion Sooner and Curly never got a chance to lay his hands on him. If he and Marion ever partnered up, that ole bull might still do what he had been purchased to do. But that would be something he would think about later. Right now, he needed time to get himself together, and what better way to do that than to get back into ranching and seeing what he could do to help the Senora put her place back together. The land here was not just big, it was huge and he would be challenged. Even the sky looked big, just like it did back in Texas.

Clay wondered what he'd let himself in for as the big stallion trotted along at a steady gait, keeping up with the buggy. Suddenly Clay realized he would not just be going back to ranching dealing with bandits again, and he wasn't sure how he felt about that. That would more than likely mean using his gun.

They were half way down into the valley and Clay was about to mention an idea that was forming in his mind, when the black stallion snorted and his ears went forward, just as several Mexican riders charged out of a ravine with drawn pistols.

Preoccupied with his thoughts, he'd let his guard down. His hand reached for his pistol too late. Ten pistols were pointed at him.

"Esta bien, it is alright!" the Senora yelled, holding up her hand toward the men pointing guns at them.

Clay had drawn his pistol anyway and had a bead on the lead rider.

"These are some of my vaqueros. Please, do not shoot them," she said to Clay as the riders eyed him cautiously.

Clay pulled the stallion to a halt next to the buggy and slowly returned his pistol to its resting place on his hip, watching to see what they were going to do, ready to draw and take down as many as he could if any one of them started shooting.

"Ramon, put your pistol away and come and meet our new Segundo," Victoria said with a broad sweep of her hand.

The vaqueros put their pistols away continued to eye Clay with distrust. He was a gringo and they had no reason to trust gringos – not after what Curly and his men had done. What had gotten into the Senora's head, they wondered?

Ramon, a man with pride written in his eyes, looked hard at Clay to Victoria he said, "Pardon' Senora. Are you replacing me with this, gringo, an outsider who does not know our way or speak our language? Have I done something to displease you?"

To their surprise, Clay said, "Yo hablo espanol. I speak your language somewhat and know many of your ways."

Ramon glared at Clay and started to say something Clay interrupted him. "I didn't know I would be replacin' anyone when I accepted the Senora's offer, and I sure don't want to start off on the wrong foot. Maybe we can work together. Seems like there are problems enough already without us buttin' heads."

Ramon rode over next to Clay and held out his hand. "It is possible I acted without thinking, Senor'. There is much to talk about between you and me."

Clay shook his hand and saw the strong possibility of an alliance in the man's eyes. He would need all the help he could get and it wouldn't be good to start off on the wrong foot.

"You will both dine with me this evening. We have much to discuss," Victoria said as she slapped the reins down on the horse's rear end. The horse jumped and started off at a lope, leaving them in a cloud of dust.

"So, tell me," Clay said as he and Ramon rode side by side just beyond the trail of dust the buggy was leaving, "What is the biggest problem we need to take care of first?"

"This is a large ranchero and needs many riders because of the banditos, we now have only a few. What cattle we have are kept in various small valleys spread throughout the mountains and hidden valleys. Since there are so few of us and the cattle are scattered here and there, it is very difficult to keep watch on them. The Comancheros know this and take advantage of the situation. We have gone to check on the cattle only to find the valley empty. The Comancheros are taking the cattle to Mexico and destroying the ranchero, poco un poco, little by little. Plus, we have two men, gringos, who were hired for their guns to help fight off the banditos they are lazy and never around when the banditos come. In my opinion, they are worthless."

Clay looked at the young man and saw the intensity in his eyes. "Thank you, these are the kinds of things I need to know. And yes, that would be the way to do it, steal the cattle little by little and drive them across the border into Mexico. There is no way to track them, or even say for sure who did the rustlin'," Clay said to Ramon, who nodded his head in agreement.

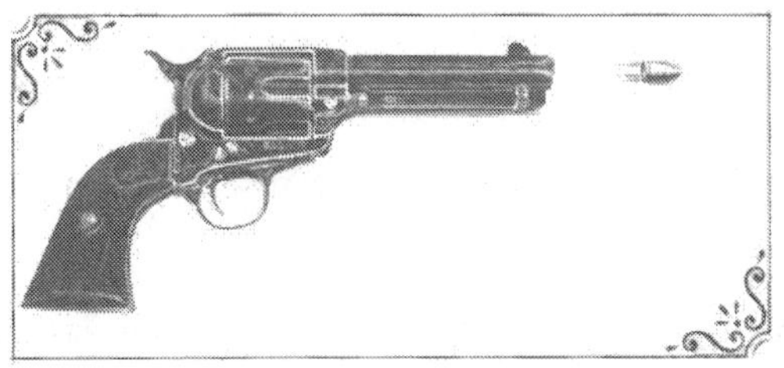

CHAPTER SIX

-

The Senora was waiting for them on the porch of the hacienda when Clay and Ramon rode up and dismounted. Ramon tied his roan at the hitch rail, while Clay just dropped the reins of the black stallion.

'That is some horse,' Ramon thought he said nothing.

Looking around, Clay realized the place was much bigger than it had looked from up near the mesa. The house was a large, two story affair, with a porch that spread all the way across the front. The floor of the porch was about ten feet wide and covered with flagstone. A small table and four chairs sat facing the west.

The barn, bunkhouse and several other buildings were inside the compound, all surrounded by the wall that had ladders on the inside and a walkway where men could stand to shoot over the top or through the slits if they needed to defend the place. It had been well thought out and had taken a lot of time, money and men to build. This was not some here today, gone tomorrow operation he found himself involved with.

When the Senora escorted them inside, Clay found the interior of the hacienda just as impressive and several degrees cooler than outside. He felt a light breeze coming from somewhere, weaving its way throughout the house. The main entry was a large room with couches and chairs, and a large fireplace in the center. A wide set of stairs led to the upper portion of the house where a walkway went all the way around in both directions, leading to the upper rooms.

A short, heavyset woman of about fifty rushed into the room and over to her mistress.

"There will be three for dinner, Anna," Victoria said to the Mexican woman, who curtsied, then hurried out of the room.

Victoria ushered them to the couches and offered them each a glass of wine, then sat down nearby in a large leather covered chair that seemed to swallow her up. Addressing Ramon, she said, "I know you have many questions." After taking a sip of her wine, she continued. "All your questions will be answered in due time for now, Ramon, you will remain bunked where you are in the Segundo's rooms."

Ramon nodded his head as the Senora continued. "Senor' Brentwood will occupy the lower bedroom at the back of the main house."

Clay noticed Ramon giving the Senora a questionable look said nothing allowing his mistress to continue. "I know that you and the others question why I would hire a man from the outside as Segundo – and a gringo, at that."

Ramon just stared at the Senora, while Clay studied Ramon.

After another sip of wine, she said, "Today, while I was in town, this man, Senor' Clay Brentwood, rode into town, got down off his horse and walked around killing Senor' Beeler and all of his men, then got back on his horse and rode away without saying a word. When I found out that he is not a gunfighter a rancher avenging the death of his wife and unborn child, who were killed by Senor' Beeler and his gang of cutthroats, I knew he would be the one who could help us."

Ramon turned and looked at Clay. "This is true, Senor'? You rode into town, got off your horse and then walked around killing Senor' Beeler and his men?"

Clay looked at the floor for a moment, and then looked Ramon in the eyes and said, "I reckon that's a fair description of what happened."

To say Ramon was flabbergasted would be stating it mildly. "Senor', you must be a very brave man."

Clay finished off his glass of wine and looked around the room. After a moment of reflection, he said, "No, bravery had nuthin' to do with it. I had an anger inside me that had been festerin' for better than two years. When I finally caught up with Curly and his gang of hard-cases, I did what I had vowed to my dead wife ta do. And when they were all in hell where they belonged, there wasn't any reason to hang around. So, I just rode out, headin' for nowhere in particular. And that's when I met up with the Senora. She was kind enough to offer me a job and I said yes. That's about all there is to it."

That was the longest string of words Clay had put together in quite some time.

Ramon looked at the Senora and asked, "If Senor' Beeler and his gang are no longer a threat to us, why do we need a man like Senor' Brentwood?"

Clay looked at the Senora, wondering the same thing.

Victoria looked at both men and smiled. She took a small sip of wine, and then said, "Yes, it is true Senor' Beeler is no longer a threat what of the Comancheros who still sneak in at night and steal our stock? And what of the gringo banditos that come through, looking for cattle or horses to steal?"

Ramon shrugged his shoulders and looked toward the window.

The Senora looked at Ramon, knowing his disappointment at not being Segundo and felt sorry for him. "Besides being very good with a gun, Senor' Brentwood knows about horses and cattle and running a ranch. He can be a big help making our ranchero become a profitable business again. I think the cattle buyers will not try so hard to take advantage of another white man. I believe we can all learn from Senor' Brentwood."

Ramon could see the wisdom in the Senora's words decided to give it one more try. "What about the others?" he said, pointing toward the door. "I do not think they will like a gringo telling them what to do?" he said. Then, glancing at Clay he said, "No offense, Senor' so much has happened."

Clay grinned and said, "None taken."

"Will I always need to be close by to translate for him and give him support?" he asked, looking directly at Victoria.

Clay patted Ramon on the shoulder. "No, mi amigo. Es no problemo, Se habla Espanol."

Once again, Ramon was taken back. "Si, yes, I remember now. Out on the trail you told me you speak our language, Senor'. But how did you come to do that?"

"I had several Mexicans working for me on my ranch in Texas. I learned from them. Fortunately, they were not around the day Curly showed up or they would also be dead. They now work for a friend of mine, Marion Sooner. He's teaching them English and they're teaching him and his wife, Mexican."

The Senora stood up and spoke to Ramon. "While you call the men together, I will show Senor' Clay to his room and we will meet you in front of the hacienda in a few minutes."

Ramon nodded his head and left the room. Clay reached down and picked up the saddlebags lying next to his chair and then stood up. "After you, boss," he said making a motion with his hand.

Clay was greatly impressed by his room. Not only was it very large, twenty by twenty feet - but also well furnished. Against one wall was a bed large enough to hold three of him. On another was a large, four-legged closet to hang his clothes in, with a tall dresser next to it for other things. Across from the foot of his bed was another dresser, with a tall mirror for grooming standing next to it. And at the end of the bed, was a box for sitting on while he put on his boots. Two French doors with six glass windows each made up a portion of the bedroom wall. On either side of the doors, were bookshelves filled with books printed in English - Shakespeare, Keats and other famous authors from around the world. In front of one of the bookshelves was a rocking chair where he could relax and read. A small patio with a wooden table and two chairs sat just beyond the patio doors, where he could sit in the evening and enjoy some peace and quiet.

Clay had never had a room this nice in his entire life and he stood for a long moment, admiring it.

"I hope the room is to your liking."

"Senora. . . err, ah, Victoria, I'm overwhelmed to say the least. I can't imagine not being comfortable here," he stammered.

She looked at the saddlebags he was holding and asked, "Where are the rest of your things?"

"This is it. I've lived on the move for the past couple of years and didn't need much. I'll see to gettin' some things as soon as I have time to go to town."

He tossed the saddlebags on the bed and turned to his new boss. "But right now, I'd like to get acquainted with the men."

She smiled and said, "I thought you might. They'll be waiting out front," and with that she turned and left the room with Clay just a couple of steps behind her.

As they walked toward the front of the house where Ramon and the others were waiting, Clay could not help noticing the sway of the Senora's hips and the effect it was having on him.

He quickened his step and caught up to her. Walking side by side with her was a lot easier on his nerves and imagination.

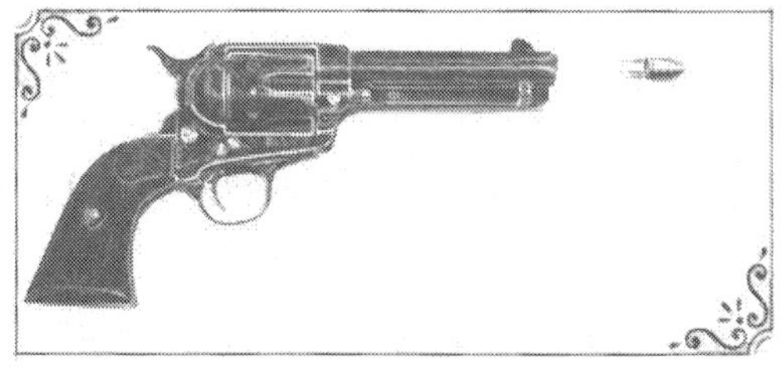

CHAPTER SEVEN

-

The men who worked for the Senora were standing around, mumbling to each other, wondering what kind of man this gringo the Senora had hired would be? If he was anything like the two pistoleros the Patron had hired, there would be much trouble. They each hoped he would not. Some were voicing their opinions in whispers.

Ramon had told them he was as surprised as they were said nothing else.

And why was Ramon not their new Segundo, they all wondered? Everyone liked Ramon, even though he was young and had much to learn.

The men looked up as the Senora and the gringo came out the front door of the hacienda. In respect for who she was, they pulled off their sombreros as she stepped to the edge of the porch.

She stared at them for a moment, and then cleared her throat. "I know you are all wondering why I hired this man to be your new Segundo instead of promoting Ramon," she said in Spanish.

The men looked down at the ground. Some of them twisted the brims of their hats none of them said anything. After all, she was the Senora and she could do as she pleased.

"This man," she said, pointing toward Clay, "single-handedly, shot and killed Senor' Curly Beeler and his gang today - ten men - the same men who shot and killed my husband, your Patron, and several of your compadres.

There were quiet murmurs.

His name is Clay Brentwood and he is here to help us put our ranchero back on its feet. He is not only a man who is good with a pistolero he also knows ranching. I want you to work for him as you would work for me. Senor' Brentwood and Ramon will work together to make us strong again."

When the men heard that Ramon would be working with the gringo, they felt relieved and nodded their agreement, glad Ramon was still involved.

The Senora smiled and said, "I have work to do. I will leave you in his hands. Again, I expect you to welcome Senor' Clay Brentwood and follow his instructions as you would mine."

With that, she turned, smiled at Clay and headed back inside. As she passed him she said, “They’re all yours. Work with them, they are all good men.”

Clay stepped up next to Ramon, who was standing just off the porch. He looked at the men for a moment, and then said, “Hola. Me nombre es Clay Brentwood.”

At first, they were surprised when their new Segundo spoke to them in their own language and soon felt comfortable with him as he lined out who he was and what he would expect from them, and how he and Ramon would work together to once again make this a paying ranchero. He also said they needed more men and would look to them to make recommendations from people they knew.

They all smiled and nodded their heads, happy not to be hiring more outsiders.

After a few minutes, Clay turned to Ramon and asked, “Where are the two white men you said were hired for their guns?”

“Ah, you mean the pistoleros, Frank Cushin and Harley Grimm?”

“If that’s their names? Yeah. I don’t see any white men among these men.”

“No, Senor’. That is because today is payday and they have gone into town to drink their fill. They will come riding in later today looking to eat their evening meal. They will eat, drink some more, and then sleep until midday tomorrow.”

“I see,” said Clay. “If you see ’em before I do, let me know.”

“Oh, I think you will notice them when they return. They will be drunk, loud and shooting off their pistolas.”

"I'll keep my eyes and ears open," Clay said. "If you don't mind, see that the men go about their regular duties. I need a couple of minutes to put my things away, then you and me can have us a pow-wow."

"Si, Senor'. If that means a talk, then yes, we need to have, as you say, a pow-wow."

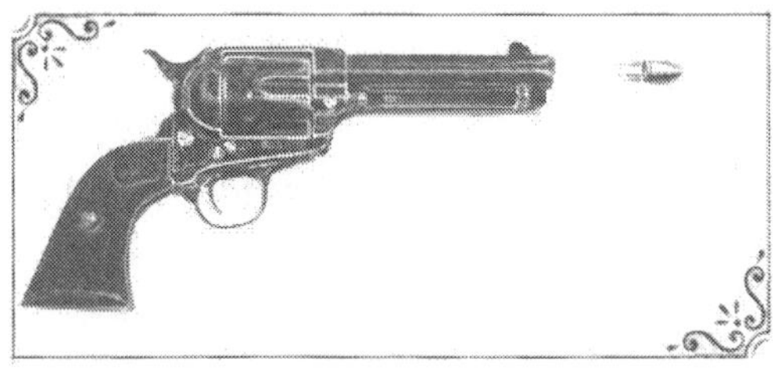

CHAPTER EIGHT

The rest of the day went by smoothly. Clay and Ramon rode to the top of the mesa where they could see for a long way in all directions. The expanse was almost enough to take his breath away. Clay imagined it looked just as it had thousands of years ago, when the mountains and mesas sprang from the ground during the time of creation. He could imagine the earth rumbling, lightning flashing and these great pieces of rock pushing their way toward the stars. The big stallion pawed the ground and shook his head as though he was feeling the same things Clay was.

Clay patted his neck. "I know, big fella, I know."

Ramon told in great detail how Victoria's husband, the Patron, had married her just to get his hands on the ranchero. Victoria's father had not been a good gambler and Santiago Ontiveros got him drunk and suckered him into a fixed horse race, with the prize being marriage to his daughter, the beautiful Senorita Hernandez. Two weeks after the wedding, Senor' Hernandez was found out on the desert, shot in the back. The new Patron told them rustlers had killed him, and the following day, he took over.

Clay got the impression Ramon hadn't been any too happy with his new Patron and asked, "What was he like to work for?"

Ramon looked around to make sure no one else could hear, then said, "He was not a good man and knew nothing about ranching bossed us around like we were peons and he was the King of Spain."

"Do you think he had any dealings with the Comancheros?"

Ramon looked off in the distance for what seemed a long time. "I do not know, Senor' Clay many of us thought it might be. He would be gone for a day or two and return with his pockets filled with money. He always told the Senora he had won it from gambling."

"Then why did the Comancheros want to kill him?"

"It was Senor' Beeler and his men who shot him, not the Comancheros."

"I see," Clay said as he rolled and lit a cigarette. "Curly would shoot a man just because he didn't like the look of him or because sometimes he just felt like killing somebody."

"This was a very good ranchero when the old Patron was alive. He knew about ranching and took good care of his people." Ramon pulled a small cigarillo from his shirt pocket and lit it. "I hope you are that kind of man, Senor'."

Clay looked over at Ramon, then off toward the vastness of the land and finally said, “So do I, Ramon. So do I.”

The sun was nearing the western horizon when Clay and Ramon rode through the gates of the hacienda. The men had finished their work, had their supper, and were lounging next to the well. Three of them had guitars and were serenading anyone who would listen, which seemed to be most of the men, women and children who lived on the ranchero.

As Clay and Ramon rode up, the playing and singing stopped and the people turned and looked at their new Segundo.

“Don’t stop on my account,” Clay called out as he stepped down from the big horse and dropped the reins. “That sounded mighty pretty. Keep playing. They say, music is good for the soul,” he said in their own tongue.

The men began to play and sing again and the people relaxed. Two couples got up and began to dance. Clay was watching them with a smile on his face and turned his head just as Ramon reached for the black stallion’s reins.

The big horse swung its head, eyes wide and nostrils flaring and tried to take a bite out of Ramon’s hand. Fortunately, Clay reached out and laid a hand on the black stallion’s neck and said, “Whoa there big fella, he’s a friend.”

Ramon jumped back and said, “I was only going to put him in the barn for you, Senor’.”

“I know, and I thank you he’s not good with strangers. It’s just been him and me for a long time, and now I’m the only one he’ll let do for him.”

Everyone close to the well had seen what happened and learned a lesson. Do not go near Senor' Clay's black stallion.

Clay had just finished rubbing down the big horse and turned him into the stall when he heard off key singing and the sound of two pistols being fired. He poured some oats into the trough and then pitched in a fork full of hay before he headed for the open doors of the barn.

The people near the well were gone. Like smoke disappearing into the night, they had vanished. Clay watched as the two drunken white men climbed clumsily off their horses and staggered toward the building where everyone who worked for the Senora, had their meals.

One of them, a tall man with a hallow voice yelled out, "Jose, get us somethin' to eat and be quick about it or I'll shoot yer foot off!"

Clay noticed that the wick on a lamp was suddenly turned up and a heavyset Mexican man opened the door and stepped back.

"He's been waiting for them because he's afraid of them," Clay mumbled to himself as he headed in their direction.

From a window where she could watch without anyone seeing her, the Senora peeked from behind a curtain, wondering how her new Segundo would handle the two white men? She had tried to fire them but they had just laughed at her.

Also, from hidden places, the people watched - some making the sign of the cross.

"Hold up there," Clay called out, as the two drunks were about to enter the door.

Both men turned and stared at the white man who walked up and stopped just a few feet from them.

"Who the hell are you?" the shorter of the two asked.

"I might ask you the same question," Clay answered in an even tone.

Suddenly they didn't seem so drunk any more. "I'm Frank Cushin," said the tall man, letting his gun hand drop to just above the butt of his pistol.

"And I'm Harley Grimm," the shorter one boasted. "We're the pistoleros around here so you better watch yer mouth, mister."

"Were. You were the so-called pistoleros not anymore. Besides, the way I hear it, the only thing you were good at was shootin' off your mouths."

The two men looked at each other with questioned looks.

Frank stepped in front of Clay, flexing the fingers of his gun hand. "Are you prepared to back up that statement, or is your mouth bigger than your brag?"

Harley stepped just a few feet to the left of Frank, his gun hand twitching. "Any time you're ready, mister."

"Guess you think you're real tough when it's two against one or shootin' a man in the back," Clay said as the moon came creeping over the mesa, lighting up the area.

"You got a big mouth on you mister. Get ready to draw!"

Clay laughed. This was like something you'd read in one of those dime novels. His eyes narrowed and he said, "Your call."

Both men went for their guns but before either one could clear leather Clay had the drop on them. He could have killed them where they stood he didn't.

Frank was the first to speak. "You're pretty fast ole son how are you with your fists?"

"Just what I was hopin' you'd ask," Clay answered. "Why don't you boys unbuckle them holsters - let 'em drop, and then we can find out."

Clay's ease of manner un-nerved them and they were hesitant until Clay threw them a challenge they couldn't refuse.

"What's the matter, you two afraid of fightin' a lone man nearly twice your age? Instead of callin' you Frank and Harley, I guess I'll have to call you, chicken and coward."

"Nobody calls me that and gets away with it, mister. I'm gonna beat on you until you beg me ta shoot ya," Frank said as he unbuckled his gun belt and let it drop.

Harley followed Frank's lead and did the same. The two men, sober now, began to circle Clay until Frank was in front of Clay and Harley was directly behind him.

Clay grinned and asked, "That the way you boys want it - one in front of me and one of you in back of me? I've seen some cowards in my time you two take the cake. All right if that's how you want it, so be it. Now that you boys are in position, do we fight now or do you want to continue dancin'?"

Clay could hear Harley's breathing as he rushed up from behind to hit him in the back of the head. At the same time, Frank closed in with a roundhouse swing at Clay's head.

Just before either one landed a blow, Clay stepped to the side and watched as the two men collided, knocking each other to the ground.

As they climbed to their feet, Clay said, "I thought you two wanted to beat up on me, not each other."

With balled fists and fire in their eyes, the two men circled Clay, looking for an opening.

Finally, Clay asked, “Are we gonna fight or just circle each other until we get dizzy and fall down?”

This was more than Frank could take and he rushed Clay and smashed him on the jaw, sending Clay back a couple of steps.

“Now, that’s more like it,” Clay said as he threw a right into Frank’s stomach and watched him fold over, spewing foul smelling beer onto the ground as he gasped for breath.

From behind, again, Harley smashed Clay over the head with a club he’d found somewhere.

Stunned not out, Clay whirled and looked at Harley who had stepped back, the club poised high above his head. “And I thought you boys were supposed to be tough. You hit like ah woman. Now I’m gonna show you what it feels like to be hit by a man,” Clay said as he stepped forward.

Harley dropped the club and turned to run Clay caught him by the shoulder and spun him around, then began a series of jabs and short shots at the man’s head and body; not enough to put him down hard enough to break some ribs, his nose and jar a few teeth loose.

Harley was staggering around, wishing the man would stop. He was in more pain than he’d ever been in, in his entire life. Raising his hands in defeat, he plopped down on his rear, trying to figure out how to breathe - his broken ribs screaming out with pain.

By now, Frank had his wind back and jumped onto Clay’s back and began hitting him on the head. Clay raised his arm up and drove his right elbow into Frank’s rib cage, knocking the man loose.

Frank was holding his ribs with one hand and trying to swing his other fist at Clay but wasn’t having any success because every time he missed, Clay smashed Frank in the face, until Frank's eyes were swollen almost closed.

When Frank had enough, he raised his hands in defeat, and asked again, "Who the hell are you?"

Clay picked up their gun belts and began emptying the shells from the cylinders. "I'm the new Segundo and you're both fired. You've got ten minutes to get your gear and get off this ranch. If I see you on the property again, I'll figure you're up to no good and shoot you down for cattle rustlers, and then leave your carcasses for the coyotes ta feed on. Do I make myself clear?"

Without a word, Frank and Harley staggered to their horses. Struggling because of their broken ribs, they finally hauled themselves into their saddles. Near the front gate, Frank called over his shoulder, "You'll hear from us again, Mister Segundo."

"Whenever you feel like another beatin', com'on back," Clay yelled, watching them hightail it through the gate, holding their sides.

As the two men rode toward town, Clay wondered if he was going to need eyes in the back of his head. There were a lot of places out there where a man could get ambushed from and these two were not above such tactics.

Ramon, followed by the rest of the residents, came filing out from their hiding places. One of the guitarists began playing and making up a song about Clay.

Ramon walked over and reached out his hand. "You have done a good thing for us this day, my new friend I am afraid you have made bitter enemies of those two gringos. They may be lazy and drink too much do not under estimate them. They are like snakes and will strike when you least expect them to."

Before Clay could make a reply, the Senora walked up and asked, "Are you alright?"

Clay rubbed the back of his head and felt a small lump. "Couple of small bruises here and there nuthin' serious. Wasn't much of a fight when you get right down to it.

Deep down, they're both cowards and we're better off with them gone."

"Come inside and let me see to your wounds," the Senora said in a soft voice.

The music and dancing started up again as Clay and the Senora walked toward the hacienda. Whispers about their new Segundo were being tossed back and forth.

Sitting on a chair in the kitchen, sipping on a small glass of brandy, while Victoria nursed his wounds, made Clay glad he'd accepted her job offer. Not only was she beautiful she smelled nice too – like lilacs in the spring. They could hear the music coming from outside. The man was still singing about Clay and the pistoleros.

"I think you have been accepted as Segundo," Victoria said as she put a cold rag against the lump on Clay's head.

"Just figured the place would be better off without them two around, is all," Clay said, trying to make light of the situation.

Victoria walked around in front of Clay and leaned down and took his face in her hands. "Well I think it was more than you make of it, and I want to add my thanks for getting rid of them." And with that, she reached down and kissed him on the lips.

Clay wasn't sure what he was supposed to do, push her away or kiss her back.

Her lips were soft and the kiss tasted sweet as fresh honey and his heart began to beat faster. He didn't want it to end, so he kissed her back.

When she finally pushed herself away, her face was flushed and her breath was coming in labored gasps. She stared at him for a moment, then turned and hurried out of the room.

Clay emptied his glass of brandy, then poured himself a second one and downed it in a single pull.

After a moment, he stood up and holding the cold rag against the bump, headed toward his room, wondering what the hell just happened.

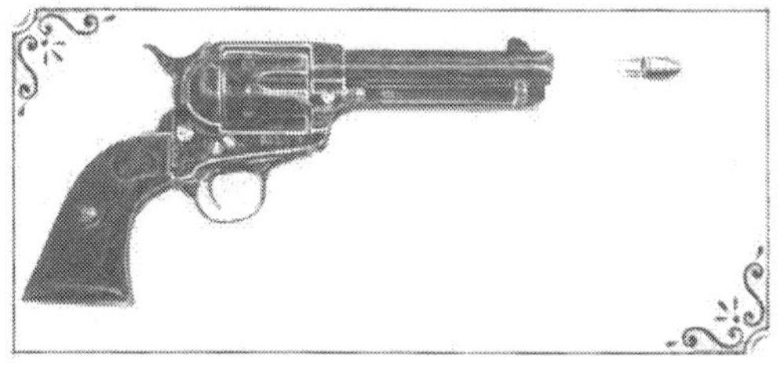

CHAPTER NINE

-

During the next three months, Clay and the Senora walked a thin line, each of them waiting for the other one to say something or make a move neither did, even though each one wanted to.

Clay wasn't sure how he was supposed to feel. The man part of him wanted to take her in his arms and make love to this beautiful young woman who had kissed him so feverishly, then ran away. But the other side of him felt guilty. After all, she had hired him to put her ranch back on its feet and that's where his priorities should lie. Plus, there was Martha, his departed wife, who was still very much a part of him.

Keeping that in the front part of his mind, he tried to concentrate solely on the work at hand.

Victoria, however, paced the floor every night. She was having a difficult time sleeping because he filled her dreams every time she closed her eyes. Several times she had been tempted to confront him. From the way he looked at her, she knew he had similar desires. Following a particularly vivid dream, she had considered slipping down to his room had restrained herself. After all, she had hired him to do a job and so far, he was more than fulfilling his obligation. The ranchero was running smoothly, the herds were growing, and there had been only one attempt to steal her cattle by some Mexicans from across the border. Clay, Ramon and a few of the new vaqueros he'd hired, tracked them down to a meadow just below the border. Two days later they came riding back with her cattle. Nothing was ever said about the banditos.

Ramon was becoming a better Segundo for being around Clay. The vaqueros looked up to Clay, while all of the women blushed when he came near. And so, their relationship was friendly businesslike. She was the boss and he was the Segundo.

The women giggled and talked amongst themselves, wondering how long it would take Senor' Clay to declare his feelings for the Senora, or she for him. Even the men were placing bets.

Of course, neither Clay nor the Senora was aware of the betting or what was said behind closed doors.

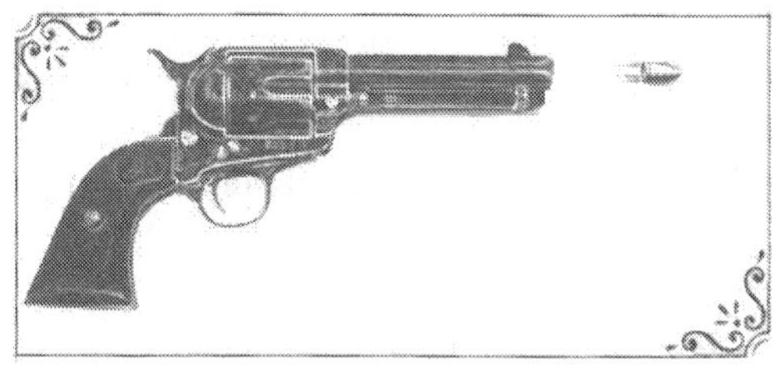

CHAPTER TEN

-

Like most days, the sky was clear the sun was a little less bright and hot. It was not yet winter the heat of the summer was behind them. Over breakfast, Clay and the Senora discussed the way things were going and she told him how pleased she was with the way the ranchero was growing. Then there was an awkward moment that made Clay nervous. She was looking particularly beautiful this morning and he found himself mumbling something about riding out to check on the new cattle – then excused himself and headed for the barn before he blurted out what he was really thinking.

An hour later, riding out across the desert, Clay was alone for the first time in several weeks and it felt good. It gave him time to reflect on things.

The black stallion loped across the desert at a leisurely pace, stretching his long legs, enjoying the freedom from the limited space of the corral.

Clay was headed for the hills in the near distance and the hidden valley with its small herd of Hereford cattle. The entrance to the valley was very narrow and nearly undetectable. But inside, the tall hills sheltered a lush valley from the harsh desert winds, making it ideal for what he had in mind.

After accidentally finding the hidden valley with its knee-deep grass and small, crystal clear lake, Clay convinced the Senora to purchase a Hereford Bull and two dozen heifers from a man back in Kansas City who agreed to ship them to Albuquerque by train. He and three vaqueros had gone to Albuquerque and herded them down to the small valley where they now were.

Clay's idea was to raise quality beef stock for the surrounding ranches and towns where now only Longhorns were found. He envisioned becoming a breeding ranch for other ranchers who wanted to better their stock, which in turn would bring the Senora a good-sized profit. They would also have young bulls for sale.

He figured this was something he knew a lot more about than gun slinging; never realizing that thought would soon be put to the test.

Clay slowed the black stallion to a walk as he pulled off his hat and wiped his forehead on his shirtsleeve. He was about to put his hat back on when he felt something smash against the side of his head in a glancing blow hard enough to drive him from the saddle. Automatically, Clay grabbed for his rifle and yelled, "Go home, boy! Go home!"

By the time the sound of the shot came rumbling across the sky, Clay Brentwood was face down on the desert floor, blood seeping from his head, creating a large spot of dark red sand. He never heard the roar of the rifle.

The two men Clay fired three months back, Frank Cushin and Harley Grimm, stood up from their hiding place and grinned at each other. Harley pulled a binocular case from his saddlebag, then removed a pair of field glasses, and lifted them to his eyes. He studied the body lying on the desert floor, carefully, and could see the growing pool of blood next to Clay's head. He lowered the glasses and said, "That's good shootin'. You got him in the head."

Frank Cushin grinned and said, "I don't reckon he'll be firin' nobody else. Think I should take another shot just ta make sure?"

Harley took another quick look, and then said, "Nah, he's dead. No use wastin' another bullet."

As he walked back to his horse and began putting the field glasses away, he said, "Guess there's nuthin' left ta do now but ride over and tell Mendoza the job is done and collect our money."

Frank nodded his head in agreement as he slid his rifle back into the boot on the right side of the saddle. "As soon as we get our money, we can hi-tail it for the border. We'll be drinkin' tequila and snugglin' up ta some pretty senoritas before the Senora finds out her Segundo has gone ta meet his maker and those new cows are missin'."

"Yeah, she'll blame his death on the banditos that stole her cows," Harley said as he stepped into his saddle.

As the two men rode away, they were laughing and in a good mood. The man who had made them look bad in front of the vaqueros had gotten his comeuppance. In this heat, the flies would already be swarmin' around, and shortly the vultures would be havin' a feast.

It had been a good day so far, Harley thought, and would get even better once they collected their money and got down into Mexico. Maybe he could talk one of them pretty senoritas ta climb in the bathtub with him?

-

When Clay opened his eyes, the sun momentarily blinded him. His head felt like it was about to bust wide open. Even though he'd lost a lot of blood, and felt weak, he knew he'd been lucky, again. He figured he must have the hardest skull west of the Mississippi. This was the second time he'd been shot in the head and was still alive to tell about it. Very slowly, Clay climbed to his knees and looked around while he waited for the spinning to stop. After several minutes, he was able to stand up, using his rifle as a crutch.

Even then, he had to wait a moment to regain his balance. Once he felt steady, he pulled the bandana from around his neck and wrapped it around his head to stop the flow of blood that was now running down into his right eye. Next, he checked his gun belt. It was full of cartridges that would fit both, his pistol and his rifle; and both weapons were fully loaded. He didn't know if it would be enough it would have to do. Hell, he wasn't even sure who had shot him he had a strong suspicion who, and why.

Twenty minutes later, Clay staggered into the narrow passageway and felt a cool breeze wash over him. He leaned against a boulder and sucked in deep breaths as he re-tied the bandana as tight as he dared. He couldn't afford to keep losing blood.

A short distance away, Clay found a place that would allow him to climb up and look around. From here, he could see both the valley and the passageway. In the valley, Clay saw a group of men rounding up the small herd of Hereford cattle.

Clay took another look around and decided this would be a good place to make a stand and tried to make himself as comfortable as he could. He figured it wouldn't be long before he was back to sending bad men to hell, again. Somehow this wasn't how he saw his future when he'd signed on with the Senora.

Not far from the cattle, Clay saw an exquisitely dressed Mexican under a wide sombrero, sitting astride a beautiful paint, talking to the two men he'd fired, Frank Cushin and Harley Grimm – the same two men who had recently shot him and left him for dead. At least that's the way he figured it.

The canyon was like an echo chamber and he could hear what they were saying, along with the bawling of the cattle and the voices of the Mexican rustlers.

Mendoza reached into his jacket pocket and pulled out a small leather pouch, then dumped some gold coins into his palm. After counting them, he handed the coins to Frank, who handed Harley his share of the blood money. "Gracias," Mendoza said.

Frank Cushin saluted Mendoza with the tip of his finger against the brim of his hat and said, "Mendoza." Then, without more words, he and his partner turned and rode toward the opening of the passageway.

Clay had heard about a Mexican bandito called Carlos Mendoza – the man came across the border, stole cattle and horses and then disappeared back into the wilds of Mexico. There was even a wanted poster of him tacked up on the interior wall of the barn, along with several others. The one about Curly Beeler had a big X across it.

Clay watched the two men ride toward him and debated whether to kill them or let them go. If he shot them now, while they were still in the passageway, it would alert the banditos and Mendoza would stampede the cattle and he would play hell stopping them. He decided to let them pass and deal with them later - if there was to be a later.

Clay didn't have long to wait before he saw the bull heading his way with the heifers trailing not far behind. The big Hereford bull seemed none too happy about leaving this small valley with its sweet grass and cool water. One of the banditos had to keep slapping him on the rump with the tip of his bullwhip.

The rest of the banditos were relaxed and laughing, not expecting any trouble. One of them was playing a guitar and singing about making love to a woman.

When the bull was about to enter the narrow passageway, Clay pointed his rifle toward the ground just in front of the big animal and pulled the trigger. The roar of the rifle rolled off the canyon walls like thunder as the bullet tore a hole in the sand just a few inches in front of the bull.

In a panic, the bull whirled around – bellowing and kicking up his heels; charging back toward the interior of the canyon, with the heifers in hot pursuit.

Clay's next bullet drove the bandito with the bullwhip out of his saddle. The man was dead before he hit the ground.

A second bandito drew his pistol and fired in Clay's direction. Clay fired a third shot and another horse had an empty saddle.

Mendoza and his men rode at breakneck speed back into the valley before he called a halt and turned back. "Who are you?" he called out. "And why are you trying to steal my cattle?" Mendoza asked in halting English with a Mexican accent.

"I'm the fella you paid those two no-goods to kill. Seems like you wasted a good bit of gold. And they ain't your cattle. They belong to Senora Ontiveros."

"You are wrong, my friend. I paid no one to kill you. And these cattle are mine. I bought them from the Senora only this morning. I have a bill of sale. Come and see for yourself."

Clay shook his head at the audacity of the man. "You and I both know that's a lie. The Senora would never sell those cattle without consultin' with me first. But seein' as how you say you have a bill of sale, I would be interested in takin' ah look at it. Why don't you come over here and show it to me? If it's all proper, like you say, you and your boys are free ta take the cattle and go," Clay yelled back.

"How do I know that I can trust you, my friend? You might keep the bill of sale and shoot me," Mendoza replied.

"First off, I ain't your friend, and second, I got no cause ta shoot anybody if they're not doin' anything wrong."

"If you have no cause to shoot anyone, why did you shoot two of my men?"

"Cause you ain't proved you ain't rustlers, yet. And if you and your men, ain't, well then, you got my apologies."

Mendoza stared at the sky while some of his men were quietly putting the small herd back together again.

Clay watched, knowing once they got them rounded up, Mendoza and his men would stampede them through the pass and he wouldn't be able to turn them back this time. Suddenly, an idea came to him. It would be a long shot he had to try or the cattle would be lost. Even if it didn't work, maybe it would buy him some time. He raised the rifle to his shoulder and took careful aim. He took in a breath of air, held it for a moment, and then let it out slowly as he squeezed the trigger. He heard the boom and felt the rifle buck against his shoulder and watched as the tip of the bull's left horn went flying off into the grass.

The big Hereford bull jumped straight up in the air and came down running for all he was worth toward the far side of the valley – the heifers right behind him.

Mendoza shook his head from side to side. "Now see what you have done! You have spoiled everything! I had thought to let you live now I see that I am going to have to kill you before I can get my cattle out of this valley."

Mendoza called over a few of his men and gave them instructions. As the men rode out in different directions, Mendoza called out. "You still have time to get away and save your life before my men get into the hills above you. When this happens, I can no longer help you. Save yourself, Senor'. I want only the cattle. Are you willing to give up your life for a few measly head of cattle that are not even yours?"

"When I hired on as Segundo, that made them my responsibility. So, I don't reckon I can just walk away and let you steal 'em," Clay called back. "It's called, ridin' for the brand."

While the banditos were climbing into the hills above him, Clay looked around for a new place from which to fight – one that wasn't so vulnerable from above. What his searching eyes found was on the other side of the passageway, which meant he would have to move further back toward the opening so he could cross without being seen.

Clay moved a hundred feet back down the passageway and just to be safe, he belly crawled to the opposite side, then made his way up to his new hiding spot.

Clay had just settled in when high up on his right he saw one of Mendoza's men pointing his pistol down in the direction where he'd just been. Clay raised his rifle to his shoulder, took a breath and slowly squeezed the trigger. The bandito lurched backward, blood spurting from his chest. Immediately, bullets began to pepper the rocks around his former hiding place.

Clay took his time, waiting for the right moment, and picked them off, one at a time, blending his shots with theirs. This time he wasn't shooting to kill. His intention was to only wound them bad enough to take them out of the fight. He hated killing men who were only following orders.

One of them must have found his new location because a bullet glanced off a rock, just missing his head. Pieces of splintered rock dug into his neck, causing him to wince and utter a couple of cuss words.

Clay scooted down. Now that they knew his location, they didn't have to see him to make a direct hit. They could bounce lead off the rocks near him and hope some of it ricocheted into his body. He knew he couldn't stay here or he would soon be a dead man.

Through a small opening between two of the rocks, Clay could see Mendoza and four of his men making their way toward him. It was coming down to a face-to-face shootout with him against Mendoza and the four men he had left.

"Hold on," Clay called out, trying to buy himself a little time. "Let me get down from here so's we can palaver."

Mendoza and his men stopped. "What is this, palaver, you talk about?" Mendoza yelled back. "I do not know, palaver."

By now, Clay had almost reached the ground and was out of sight. "It means ta talk," Clay called out with his hands cupped around his mouth, pointing in the direction where he'd been hiding in the hopes it would sound like he was still up there.

Eventually it worked because they began pounding the area with bullets.

Silently as he could, Clay climbed on down to the desert floor where he crouched behind a large boulder and waited.

A menacing sun beat down on them relentlessly as time went crawling by. If it had been Apaches, Clay would have been in even more trouble than he was. Apaches were masters at the waiting game Mendoza and his men were not Apaches. Clay watched as they jumped at every little sound. Knowing it wouldn't be long; he prepared himself for a fight. Who would win, he wasn't sure he knew it wasn't in him to just let them go.

Mendoza finally made a decision and called his men together. "I do not know if the gringo is dead or still alive we cannot remain here, trapped like animals in a cage. We will stampede the cattle and follow them through the passageway. It is our only chance."

Clay moved to a spot where he hoped he could get a shot at them as they rode past. This time he would give no quarter, especially to men who would go off and leave their wounded behind. Once the cattle started running, it would be the rustlers or him.

Clay heard the shot that started the stampede and braced his hips against the rock wall, at the same time, thumbing the hammer back on his Colt pistol. This would be close up work.

As they raced past, Clay got off two shots. Both shots missed because of the dust cloud that impaired his aim. Their returning fire tore splinters off the boulder near his face and drove small slivers of rock into his eyes.

Clay squatted down to further hide himself, trying not to scream out in pain and reveal his position.

CHAPTER ELEVEN

-

Less than a minute after they'd gone by, Clay heard gunfire and shouting, then nothing but the sound of cattle bawling. He remained silent and waited.

Suddenly, out of the silence, he heard a woman's voice call out. "Senor' Brentwood, it is I, Victoria Ontiveros. Where are you? Are you injured?"

"I'm over here!" Clay called out – overjoyed to hear her voice.

The next thing Clay knew, she was holding him close to her and he could smell her sweetness.

As she held him close and stroked his hair, she whispered, "When your horse came running into the yard and your rifle scabbard was empty, I knew you had trouble. I was afraid something terrible had happened to you. You told me you would be coming here to check on the cattle, so I called the vaqueros together and we came as fast as we could. We captured the bandito Mendoza and his men as they came out of the passageway with the cattle."

Clay smiled and relaxed some for the first time since he got shot in the head. "That's good ta hear," he said.

Pushing away far enough to examine him as she talked, she said, "Some of our vaqueros are rounding up the cattle and will return them to the valley. The others will take Mendoza and his men to the new sheriff in town."

Our vaqueros? Clay wondered as he lifted his head.

When the Senora saw his face, she exclaimed, "You're bleeding! Why didn't you say something?"

"Ain't nuthin' much," Clay drawled. "Mendoza hired those two no-goods I fired awhile back and one of 'em gunshot me in the head from ambush, then later, during the shootout, I got some rock splinters in my neck and eyes. But other than that, I reckon I'm alright. There are still a few of his men up in the hills that I wounded during the fracas. I tried ta stop them there was just too many of them," he said just before everything went black.

Sometime later, Clay tried to open his eyes but found them bandaged tightly and to his surprise, they didn't hurt. With his left hand he reached up and found a second bandage wrapped around his head, and realized his head didn't hurt, either. In fact, his whole body felt light and a bit tingly.

After a moment, he realized he was no longer in the passageway to the small valley in a nice, soft bed!

Victoria Ontiveros arose from the chair she'd been sitting in for the past several hours and hurried to Clay's side. "I'm glad to see you are finally awake. How do you feel?" she asked in a voice that sounded to Clay, like it came from far away.

Clay felt himself grinning. "I can't remember feelin' better."

The Senora laughed. "That would be the laudanum the doctor gave you. He said it would take away the pain. He also said we have to be careful because laudanum can become habit forming. He also said he thinks your eyes will be as good as new in a few weeks."

"And my head?" Clay asked.

The Senora laughed again, this time long and hard. "The doctor said not to worry about your head, it is as hard as a piece of iron."

"Ah few weeks before I can get back to work, is that what the doctor said?" Clay asked.

"Yes, a few weeks. He said he will come by to check on you and change your bandages every few days."

Clay nodded his head, wondering if that meant he would be lounging in this soft bed or sittin' in the rocking chair, reading, until he was on his feet again?

It was like the Senora could read his mind because her next words were, "You will remain here in your room where I can keep an eye on you until the doctor says you are on your feet, again. If you feel you need to get up and get some exercise, I will go with you."

She placed her hand on his arm and he felt the electricity clear down to his toes.

"Are you hungry?" she asked.

"Well, now that you mention it, ah steak with some taters and beans, and maybe a cup of coffee would taste mighty good about now."

Tears formed in Victoria's eyes as she smiled and squeezed his arm, and then called out, "Anna!"

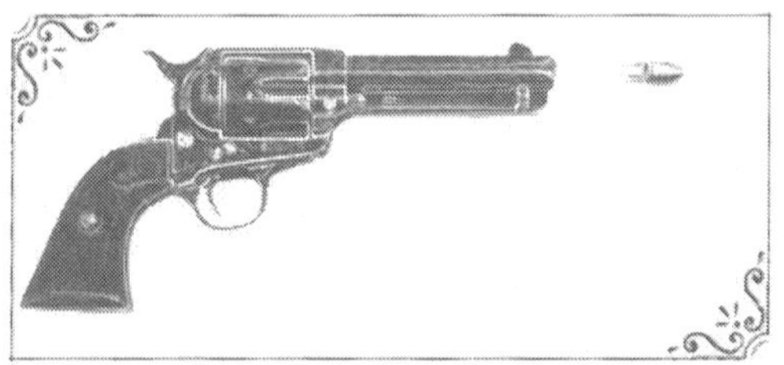

CHAPTER TWELVE

-

It had been twelve days since the doctor had confined him to his bed. He knew because every day, at least five times a day, he had asked someone how long it had been. And now, finally, he would at last be getting the bandage off his eyes the question remained. Would he be able to see?

The doctor took his time and had the Senora close the curtains in front of the double door windows leading out to the patio, to darken the room. He said he wanted to brighten the room gradually so Clay's eyes would get used to the light in small doses.

Along with the doctor, the Senora, Ramon, and Anna were in the room, every one of them anxious to see if Clay would see again none of them more worried than Clay himself. He didn't know if he could handle being blind. What would he do? He could partner up with Marion and teach him the horse business, he guessed. He wondered what Marion would think about having a blind partner? He sure couldn't stay on here as Segundo.

"You know," the doctor said as he began to unwrap the bandage, "there's no guarantee that you'll see again I'd say your chances are better'n fifty percent. In all my years of treatin' folks, I've seen several eye injuries that was worse than yours and they came through alright."

The doctor removed the last bit of bandage and stepped back and said, "alright, open yer eyes kind of slow like. Just let in a little light at a time."

Clay squinted his eyes so there was just a sliver of eyeball showing. He shook his head. "Can't see anything yet, doc."

"That's alright. Take your time. Keep opening them a little bit at a time until you can see something and then stop and tell me. We pulled the shades so it is somewhat dark in the room."

Clay continued to open his eyes until they were halfway open and he could make out a figure standing in front of him. "I think that's you I see standin' in front of me, doc."

"That's good. Yes, that's very good. Now, go ahead and open yer eyes all the way and tell me what you see."

Clay continued raising his eyelids until they were fully up. At first things were blurry then they began to clear up. He turned his head from side to side, then back at the doctor. "Well, seems like I've got ah good sized welcomin' committee. Let's see, there's you, and over there is the Senora and next to her is Anna, and over on the other side is Ramon standin' next to the curtains. How's that?"

"That's just fine," the doctor said. "Now, take a minute or two to let your eyes adjust to seeing again and when you think you're ready, we'll open the curtains a little at a time. Don't look directly at the window for now. If the light hurts your eyes, you let us know and we'll stop opening the curtains."

Clay nodded his head. "Will do."

The doctor nodded and Ramon began to open the curtains a little at a time.

Clay closed his eyes and opened them again and the first thing he saw was the face of Victoria. She was smiling and tears were running down her cheeks and dripping off her chin. She reached up with a handkerchief and wiped them away more came.

Clay wasn't sure what to say so he swung his head to look at the others. By the time Ramon had opened the curtains all the way and the room was filled with sunlight, Clay realized he felt no pain. "Ya did real good, Doc. I can see just fine and there ain't no pain. Should I look at the windows, now?"

The doctor was smiling. "Yes, do it slowly, not all at once."

Clay swallowed and then slowly turned his face toward the double door windows and saw Ramon standing there, grinning like a kid who'd gotten the Christmas present he asked for. And when the light didn't hurt his eyes, he said, "Ramon, what are you grinning at? Ain't you got work you should be doin'?"

Ramon knew his friend was joshing with him. He stepped over and rapped his knuckles on the window pain and the next thing Clay saw was the vaqueros, their wives and children, standing in front of the windows. The men had taken their hats off and the women were smiling and waving at him.

Clay got a lump in his throat and for a moment, he held his breath so he wouldn't begin to cry, too. It wouldn't look good for their Segundo to be bawlin'.

Later that day, during the evening meal, Clay looked around the table and felt a chill run down his back. Everything looked fuzzy. He shook his head and blinked his eyes.

"Is something wrong?" Victoria asked with real concern in her voice.

"No, everything is just fine," Clay said as his eyesight returned to normal.

"Are you sure?" she asked, staring at him, not quite sure she believed him.

"Really, everything is fine. I guess I'm still a bit amazed that things turned out so well," he said, hoping she believed his lie. When in truth, everything going blurry scared the Bee-Jesus out of him.

What if he was out somewhere by himself, fending off bandits and went blind? These and other thoughts he didn't want to think about ran through his mind as he looked down the table at the faces of the Senora and Ramon. Clay grinned, trying to show them that nothing was wrong.

After supper, Clay went out and sat next to the well and listened as one of the men sat on the edge of the well and played his guitar and sang sad songs about lost loves. At one point, Clay asked him to play something lively, and he did to the delight of the others who got up and danced and made happy sounds.

The moon was up and Clay felt fatigue settling in. Tomorrow would be a big day. They would be branding the new calves. He heaved himself to his feet and waved to everyone as he headed for his room. "Better get some rest, ah lot of brandin' ta be done tomorrow," he said, and watched as they nodded their heads and began to move away.

Just as he reached for the door latch of his room, the world began to swirl. He grabbed the doorframe to steady himself. Everything was fuzzy, again. Feeling his way, he staggered to his bed and dropped onto it, almost in a panic. He closed his eyes and willed himself to not think about it. The next thing he realized was bright light coming through the windows of the double doors leading out to the patio.

He blinked his eyes and sat up. Everything was clear and there was no pain but something inside him told him things were not as they should be. As he washed his face and combed his hair before going to breakfast, he decided he would ride into town and talk with the doctor. Maybe he could shed some light on what was going on.

Breakfast was about as he figured it would be; questions about how he felt. Was his sight back to normal? Was he in any pain?

Clay answered each question with just enough truth to satisfy them and after breakfast, he announced he would be taking the black stallion out for some exercise while Ramon and the others began the branding.

Both, Victoria and Ramon volunteered to ride along to keep him company, just in case he had a relapse.

Because he was headed in to see the doctor, and not out on the range, he thanked them and said, "After bein' cooped up for such a long spell, I reckon I could use some alone time, ta clear my head, so ta speak."

With worried looks on their faces, they gave in he could see they were none too happy about it.

The big stallion was glad to see Clay and showed it by nipping him on the shoulder and began dancing around as Clay rubbed his back with a rag he found hanging on the top rail of the stall. When Clay led him out and began to saddle him, the big horse stamped his feet like a young, excited colt.

When Clay stepped into the stirrup, it was all he could do to keep the big horse from bolting. The black stallion was ready and eager to stretch his legs.

The first mile or so was ridden in the direction of the cattle herds as soon as he was out of sight of the hacienda he turned the big horse toward town and gave him his head.

Clay felt the horse's muscles ripple as the black stallion leaped forward, his legs reaching out, eating up the miles. It felt good to be under the wide-open sky once again, breathing the fresh New Mexico air. Only when he felt the horse had had a good run did he settle him down to an easy lope. The run had been good for both of them. Being able to see again was a wonderful feeling; but the episode last night scared him.

All during the ride, Clay kept looking here and there to make sure things were still clear and in focus. When he reached the outskirts of town, he slowed the stallion to a walk.

Once again, the big horse danced his way down the dusty street in the direction of the doctor's office. People he didn't know waved to him and he nodded back at them. Seems the people would never forget he was the man who had cleaned out the Beeler gang, single-handed.

Ramon had told him the telegraph operator had spread the word to every sheriff this side of New York within minutes after the shoot-out and he had ridden out of town.

When he reined in at the hitch-rail in front of the doctor's office and stepped down, he heard a familiar voice calling to him.

"Hey, there, Senor' Hotshot Segundo!" I reckon my aim was ah mite off the other day, only lost yer sight for ah bit that won't happen again, not at this close range. Now why don't you turn around and face me. I want to make sure you can see me while I'm callin' you out."

The muscles in Clay's jaw tightened at the sound of Frank Cushin's voice. The man who had shot him in the head and left him for dead was looking for a face-to-face shootout. He'd heard they were down in Mexico apparently not.

This was not the time, he thought to himself. Looking around, he realized he had no choice; people were standing on the sidewalk, watching and waiting. As he turned, he flipped the rawhide loop off his colt that held it in the holster.

"Neither of you was any good with your fists. And you didn't do too well at shootin' me from ambush with a rifle. So what makes you think you can best me with a six shooter at close range?" he asked, as his head began to ache and his sight began to get blurry, again, which caused him to feel like he was about to lose his balance.

"They'll be two against one this time," Harley Grimm said as he spit a gob of something putrid into the street.

By now, it was all Clay could do to keep his balance as the two men, who stood in front of him, became nothing more than a blur. He hated to end his life this way he knew he couldn't back down. Even if he couldn't see them, he knew where they were standing. As he spread his feet in preparation for the shootout, someone stepped up next to him and he heard Ramon's voice, loud and clear.

"No, Senors, it will be two against two."

Frank and Harley looked at each other as insecurity crossed their faces, and after a long, pregnant pause, Frank said, "Not today. The sun is in our eyes – wouldn't be ah fair fight."

They backed up a couple of steps and then turned and headed for the saloon.

"Are they gone, yet?" Clay whispered.

"Si, Amigo. They went back into the saloon. Your sight is gone, again, isn't it?"

"Yeah. I can't even see you. I was headed for the doctor when they showed up. I would have probably been lyin' here in the street if you hadn't come along. And speakin' of that, where the hell did you come from? You didn't just ride into town for no reason. Aren't you supposed to be brandin' cows?"

Ramon took his friend's arm and said, "Let us go see the doctor. There will be plenty of time for explanation, later."

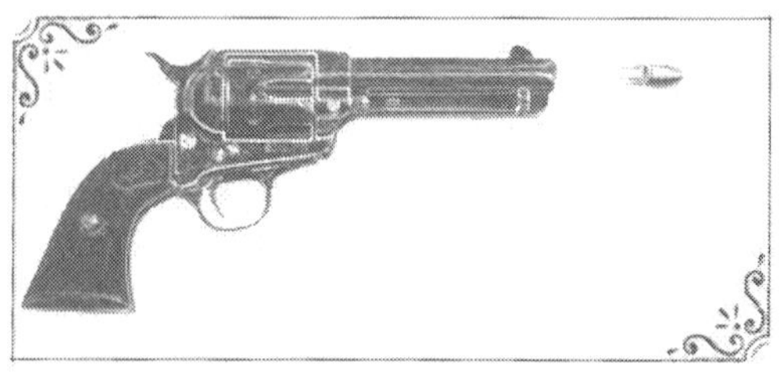

CHAPTER THIRTEEN

-

The Senora paced back and forth from one end of the hacienda to the other. Something was bothering her. Somewhere inside she knew it had to do with Clay she couldn't figure out what. He'd said he was fine and he looked all right. How long had he been gone, she wondered, as she hurried into the large front room and looked at the tall clock standing against the wall. Two and a half hours, not long if he was just out riding. There were miles and miles he could ride and just be by himself. He might even be checking the cattle.

But what if he wasn't checking the cattle? What if something was wrong? And where was Ramon? He had ridden out shortly after Clay had left. Did he suspect something and not said anything to her? This line of thinking was silly. Clay said he wanted to get out and stretch his legs and give his horse some exercise, which made sense after having such a long confinement. A man like Clay Brentwood was not the kind who could lie around in bed all day. And Ramon had said he was going to check on the cattle and the men, which also made sense. He had been Segundo during the time Clay had been laid up. And he was doing a good job. Clay had taught him well.

Then why was she pacing the floor? Her stomach told her things were not as they seemed. What if Clay was still having trouble with his eyes? What if he had gone into town to see the doctor? He had said he was fine there was a look on his face and the sound of his voice that told her he was covering up something.

She looked at the clock, again. It would be lunchtime soon and she decided to help Anna in the kitchen. Surely, they would be back by then. Plus, it would give her something to do.

Anna gave her a look when she glanced up and saw her mistress walk into the kitchen. "Worried about Senor' Clay, are you?" she asked.

Victoria hesitated. Was it that obvious? "Worried about Senor' Clay? Why should I be worried about Senor' Brentwood? Did he not tell us at breakfast that he was fine? I just thought I would give you a hand with lunch. I'm feeling a bit bored today."

"Humph," Anna muttered to herself.

"So, what are we having for lunch today?" the Senora asked as she sniffed the rich aroma floating throughout the kitchen.

"Huevos Rancheros," Anna said as she stirred the pot of chili.

"Have you gathered the eggs yet?"

Anna smiled. “Si, early this morning.”

“Oh,” the Senora said as she paced around the room.

“Have you given your horse a rub down yet today?” Anna asked, trying to figure a way to get her mistress out of the kitchen.

“No, no I haven’t,” Victoria said as she hurried toward the door. “That’s a good idea, just in case I may want to go riding after lunch.”

When her mistress was gone, Anna shook her head, “Victoria Marie Christina Claire Ontiveros, what am I going to do with you? You are hopelessly in love and don’t even realize it.”

On the way to the barn, Victoria stopped and looked off into the distance, seeing nothing but open space. As she strained her eyes, in the distance she saw a cloud of dust coming her way. Her insides filled with excitement, which didn’t last very long because she soon saw that it was only the Vaqueros coming in for the noon meal.

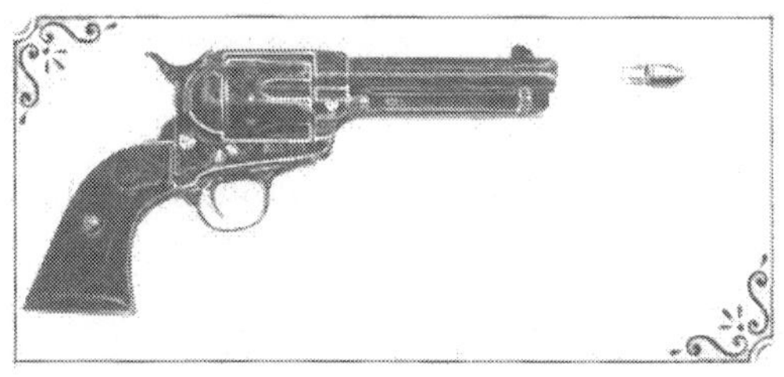

CHAPTER FOURTEEN

-

Clay sat quietly while the doctor hemmed and hawed as he peered into Clay's eyes. From time to time, he would consult a book he had laying on a nearby table.

Ramon stood silently near the door of the examining room, wondering if his friend and Segundo would ever see again. And if not, who would ramrod the ranchero? Surely not him, he wasn't ready yet, he realized for the first time.

At first, he had resented the fact the Senora had brought in an outsider – and to make matters worse, a gringo. He believed he would be Segundo after the Patron had been killed. The men liked and respected him. But running a ranchero was much different than working as a charros, which he discovered shortly after Clay took over. As the weeks went by, he realized he was not in the same class as Clay Brentwood. He didn't know the things about breeding or running a ranch that Clay did. And he was not the leader Clay was. The man knew horses and cattle, could lead men and he could be a top-notch fighter when he had to. It would not be easy to fill his boots if anything should happen to him.

Clay was trying to teach him all the things he needed to know about being a Segundo, in case something should happen to him or he decided to go back to his own ranch. He had learned much he knew he still had more to learn.

Ramon felt himself begin to sweat at the thought of running the ranchero all by himself. Yes, in the beginning, he'd wanted the job now, after riding with Senor' Brentwood…

The sound of Clay's voice interrupted his thoughts.

"Well, what's the prognosis, Doc? Will I be able to see again?" Clay asked, getting tired of all the hemming and hawing.

The doctor stepped back and pulled a small cigarillo from his pocket, then searched for a match. Taking his time, he lit the cigarillo and blew smoke into the air.

"Doc, are you there?" Clay asked.

"Yes, I'm here. And I heard your question. You want to know if you will be able to see again? Well here's the conclusion I've come to. I don't know. I just don't know. I don't know a lot about eyes, and the medical books, well, they don't tell me much."

The doctor took another puff from his cigarillo as he walked over to his desk and opened a drawer. Reaching in, he pulled out a bottle of brandy, and then looked over at Ramon. "There's three glasses in the other room. Would you be so kind?"

Ramon turned and went into the next room and returned with three glasses, which he sat on the doctor's desk. The doctor poured a small amount into each glass and handed one to Ramon, then walked over to Clay and placed a glass in his hand.

"I think I need a drink about now, and I don't like to drink alone."

As the three men sipped on their brandy, the doctor walked over and sat down on his chair near the desk. "There's a man in Kansas City who specializes in the care of eyes," the doctor said, nonchalantly. Seems he went over to Europe - Germany, I think, and studied under some feller by the name of… ah, Herman Von Somebody or other, who invented this contraption that lets you look inside a person's eye.

"Anyway, if you can afford it, I suggest you get someone to go with you and go see this man. If anyone can give you answers, he can."

"So that's it? That's your solution? I travel all the way to Kansas City to have a man tell me I'll be blind for the rest of my life?"

The doctor recognized the anger in Clay's voice and understood his feelings that was the best he could offer, except – "I guess you could stay here and stumble around trying to get from one place to another, or have someone lead you around while you feel sorry for yourself, hoping your eyesight will magically return someday."

The doctor hadn't needed to say the words out loud; for that was exactly what Clay had been thinking. "I'm sorry Doc, I didn't mean ta come down on you. I know you've done all you can. It's just that…"

"I know," the doctor said, "And I can't say I blame you. I wish I had better news for you that's the best I can offer. Hell, I don't know. Maybe your eyesight will return on its own. I've heard of that happening I just don't know. All I do know is, this fella in Kansas City is considered to be the best when it comes to eye care. And I ain't sure how much longer he'll be there. Word is, he travels around a lot, trying to help as many folks as he can. If he's still there, what have you got to lose?

"If you'd like, I can send a wire and tell him you're coming."

Clay swallowed the rest of his brandy and said, "Guess I'll have to give that some thought, Doc. How much do I owe you?"

"Nothing for the examination. But I will take two bits for the dressing I'm going to put on your eyes. I'm thinking we took the bandages off, too soon."

As the doctor was bandaging Clay's eyes, he asked, "Really think this doctor in Kansas City can help, Doc?"

"In my opinion, he's the best chance you have. You can take the bandage off in a couple of days and see if it has helped. If it doesn't, I would seriously consider being on the next train to Kansas City. Let me know and I'll send a wire."

Clay stood up and reached into his pocket and pulled out a dollar and handed it to the doctor.

"That's too much," the doctor said.

"Put the rest on account, then," Clay said, grinning. "Ramon, you still here?"

"Si, Senor'," he said stepping over and taking Clay by the arm.

"Reckon you'll have to be my eyes till we get back to the ranch," he said.

Ramon smiled and said, "No problemo, mi amigo."

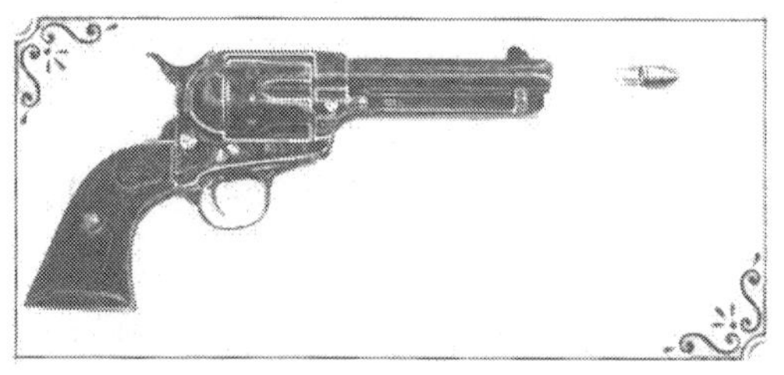

CHAPTER FIFTEEN

As Clay and Ramon stepped out of the doctor's office and headed for the livery barn, Harley Grimm stepped out of an alley and shoved the barrel of his pistol against Ramon's ribs. "Jest push them hands of yerin' in the air and stand real still Pepper Belly, or I'll blow ah hole in you big enough ta drive ah wagon through."

Both men stopped dead in their tracks and Ramon slowly raised his hands in the air as he felt his pistol being lifted from his holster.

Once again, Frank's voice filled the air. "Well now, Segundo, it looks like you ain't got no babysitter, no more. The sheriff is off on ah wild goose chase, and me, I'm gonna finish the business I was paid ta do;

ta make sure you quit takin' up breathin' space on this here planet. Now turn around and let's get to it."

Very slowly, Clay turned and faced the sound of the voice. "You sure know how to pick your time for callin' ah man out."

When Frank saw the bandages on Clay's eyes, he cursed under his breath. "Damn."

Next, he looked around and saw several people standing on the sidewalks, waiting to see what he was going to do.

After only a moment, Frank made a decision. "My contract didn't say nuthin' bout you bein' blind or sighted. The man jest said he wanted you dead and he paid me gold ta make sure you were. So here's the deal. I'm gonna count ta three and draw. Now you can stand there and take it, or, you can draw and take yer chances."

All the while Frank was talking, Clay was forming a picture in his head and had a fairly good idea where Frank was standing to make Frank a little less cautious, he turned a little bit further to his right and faced in that direction as though that's where he thought Frank was standing.

Frank saw the shift and grinned. "You ready ta meet yer maker, Segundo?"

Still facing to the right of Frank, Clay said, "Since I have no choice, I guess we may as well get it over with. Start countin' when you're ready."

One of them was about to die. And if he got lucky and killed Frank, what about Harley? Where was he standing?

Ramon wanted to warn his friend that he was facing the wrong direction but Harley had seen Clay move and then looked at Ramon and realized what he was about to do, and leaned in close and whispered. "Keep yer trap shut, Mex, if you know what's good fer ya."

Ramon nodded his head. It made no sense for both of them to die, so he held his tongue, not realizing Clay had heard Harley and had a good idea where he was standing, too.

Frank watched as Clay spread his feet a little apart and poised his hand over the grip of his pistol, while still facing the wrong direction. This was going to be easy, he thought to himself. He counted slowly, "One… two…!" Frank called out three and grabbed for his pistol before he could clear leather, he felt something slam into his chest and at nearly the same time, he heard the roar of Clay's big forty-four.

Looking over, he saw that Clay had turned and was facing him, the barrel of his pistol, smoking and pointing directly at him.

When Ramon realized what had happened, he reacted by turning away from Harley's pistol barrel and grabbing Harley's wrist in his left hand and pushing the pistol away from him, while at the same time, shoving his knee into Harley's groin. Harley reacted by screaming and doubling over with pain. As Harley fell, Ramon drove his right fist against Harley's jaw – dropping him to the dirty street. He twisted Harley's wrist and jerked the pistol from his hand, then turned to see about Clay and was surprised to see Clay facing him, with his pistol pointed in his direction.

Ramon said, "Do not worry about Senor' Harley. I have taken care of him."

By now, people were flooding the street and standing next to Clay, slapping him on the back. One man declared, "I ain't never seen the likes. Blind as a bat and you still out drew and out shot, Frank Cushin!"

People's jaws were working as fast as a windmill pump on a gusty day. There would be stories from now on about how Clay Brentwood had cleaned the town free of outlaws, twice! And the second time, blind, with patches over his eyes.

Ramon pushed his way through the crowd until he was next to his friend. “Are you alright, my friend?” he asked.

Clay felt like he was about to collapse knew he had to stay upright and not show the tension he felt. Touching his hand to his chest and feeling around, he asked, “Anybody see any blood on me, anywhere?”

“No, Senor’,” Ramon said, grinning over the roar of laughter from the crowd.

“Then I reckon I’m alright,” he said with a big grin that brought more laughter.

Over the laughter, they heard the thundering of horse’s hooves and everyone looked up to see the Senora jerk her horse to a stop, raising a large cloud of dust. She jumped off her horse and headed toward the crowd of people. The crowd parted as she ran up to Clay. “Are you hurt? I heard gunshots!”

Clay felt her hand on his arm and smelled the sweet aroma that always seemed to follow her. “Senora,” he said as he put the tip of his finger to the rim of his hat. After all, they were here in town with other folks around, and priorities had to be followed. “What brings you into town today?” he asked, kinda casual like, as if the tone in her voice and hand on his arm hadn’t already given him the answer.

Flustered, she noticed the crowd of people and was perplexed, not sure what to say. She was, after all, his boss.

Before Victoria had a chance to say anything, one of the women from town spoke up. “Those two men who your husband hired for their guns, back when times were bad, well, they were here in town today and they'd been drinking. And Frank Cushin, you know, the tall, mean one, well, when Mister Brentwood and Ramon came out of the doctor's office, Frank Cushin was waiting for them and challenged Mister Brentwood to a gunfight. And Mister Brentwood with patches over his eyes... Well, I swear; I've never seen anything like it! I almost couldn't believe my eyes."

There was a great deal of excitement in her voice as she talked. "Frank's friend, Harley Grimm sneaked up behind Ramon and stuck a pistol in his back and he couldn't do anything but stand and watch. I saw the whole thing! Mercy! I swear I've never seen the like. Even with bandages over his eyes, Mister Brentwood drew his pistol and shot Frank Cushin dead center in the chest before the man could get his pistol more than half way out of his holster and wound up shooting himself in the foot." By now, she was red faced and fanning herself. "That man certainly knows how to bring excitement to a town!"

She had the whole crowd smiling and nodding their heads - some laughing.

"Thank you, ma'am," Victoria said. "I was concerned about Mister Brentwood's eyesight. As I came into town, I heard the gunshots, and well…" she said, hoping it would satisfy the town's curiosity.

Taking hold of Clay's arm, she asked, "Where are your horses? I must get you back to the ranchero where you can rest and tell me what the doctor said."

As they were about to leave, the new sheriff came riding up and when he saw the two men on the ground, he asked, "What happened here?"

Before he knew what was happening, practically everyone in town was telling him how Clay had been called out by Frank Cushin and how, with his eyes bandaged, he still out shot the outlaw.

The sheriff pulled off his hat and was scratching his head when Clay turned toward Harley who was now standing bent over, and said, "If you want ah piece of advice, get on your horse and head for California or Colorado, anywhere I ain't; because when I get these patches off, the next time I see you, I'll send you ta be with your friend. You might want to change your line of work, cause you ain't none too good at gunfightin'."

To Ramon, Clay said, "Would you be so kind as to show the Senora where our horses are tied. I'm a bit out of sorts at the moment."

Turning again in the direction of the sheriff, Clay said, "I assume I'm free to go."

The sheriff put his hat back on his head and said, "Sure. No charges against you. I reckon you were just defending yourself. Got a whole town full of witnesses to that fact."

"Stay right here and I will bring them to you," Ramon said as he trotted off in the direction where the horses were tied.

To everyone's surprise, the sheriff got on his horse and rode down the street.

While they were waiting, the mayor walked up and presented himself. "Excuse me Mister Brentwood. I don't know if this is the right time to say anything I'm in a bit of a straight. I'm Ryan O'Field, mayor of this here town and after what just happened, our new sheriff turned in his badge and rode out. I guess this was more than he bargained for."

Clay looked in the direction of the voice and asked, "And what has that got to do with me? You think I'm the reason he left?"

"Oh no! Well… maybe not you… but the gunfight… He seemed mighty scared for some reason; didn't say a word, just gave me his badge and rode out of town."

Suddenly, everything got quiet as the mayor looked around at the folks who were standing nearby, nodding their heads, urging him on. He made a sound in his throat before he got down to business. "Harrumph. Well-sir, you see… well… what we… the whole town I mean… well… when your eyesight gets better, would you consider being our sheriff? With a man like you in charge, we'd have us a quiet little town."

Clay smiled and said, "Well now, that's a mighty nice offer I think you and the good folks have got things a mite mixed up. You think if I was sheriff this would be a quiet place ta live?"

Everyone nodded their heads in agreement.

Well that's where you nice folks are wrong. If I was sheriff, ever gun-slick this side of the Mississippi would come tryin' ta best me. We'd have more shoot-outs than you could count, and I don't think you'd want that any more than I would."

"Well now don't that beat all. I… I mean, we… we never thought of that. No Sir, you're right, that wouldn't be good for the town," the mayor said, scratching his head.

Victoria jumped into the conversation. "Mayor, I'm sure you will find a new sheriff should there ever be any trouble, like when Curly Beeler and his gang took over your town, you can count on me and my vaqueros to do what we can."

"And if I'm in the neighborhood, you can count me in, too," Clay said.

The mayor pulled off his hat and looked at the Senora. "Well now, that's real good of you both. Thank you. I'll remember that, I surely will."

About then, Ramon showed up with the horses and the three of them mounted up and rode off in the direction of the ranchero, with Clay on the black stallion, following along behind the Senora and Ramon.

Victoria was smiling to herself. She had just established herself in good standing with the town. Even without his knowing or trying, Clay Brentwood had done another good thing for the town and her.

Just outside of town, as the three of them rode abreast, Victoria looked over at Clay and asked, "Are you ever going to tell me what the doctor said? And what is this talk, if I'm in the neighborhood? Of course you'll be here. This is your home now."

Clay was silent for some time before he said anything. After lighting a cigarette and smoking close to half of it, he said, "The doctor said I should go see an eye doctor in Kansas City - some sort of eye specialist."

Victoria stopped her horse and sat there for a moment, digesting the impact and what it insinuated. She gigged her horse and rode up next to Clay. "Does what he said mean he thinks you will be blind, permanently?" She knew it was direct but she thought he would prefer it that way.

"Said he didn't know enough about eyes to say one way or another. That's why he recommended I go ta Kansas City. Said the doctor up there is supposed ta be good at helping folks with eye problems."

"Well, that settles it then. We will leave for Kansas City tomorrow. Carlos can drive us to Albuquerque in the wagon. We can catch a train from there. Thanks to you, things are quiet and running smoothly. Ramon will be able to handle things while we are gone."

Clay wasn't sure how he felt about this piece of news - just the two of them, all the way to Kansas City and back. He had to give some thought to this before he got himself in any deeper than he already was. He kicked the black stallion in the ribs and hanging onto the saddle horn, he leaned forward as the big horse leaped forward. "Let's go home, big fella."

Wind rushed past his face. Riding the black stallion at full speed and not being able to see anything - trusting the horse to know where he was going was a new experience. He could hear the thunder of hooves pounding against the dirt road as Ramon and the Senora tried to catch up.

When the black stallion finally slid to an abrupt stop, Clay could hear the laughter of children and knew they were inside the compound. As he stepped from the saddle, he heard the Senora and Ramon come up next to him and stop.

"What was that all about?" Victoria yelled as she jumped off her horse and grabbed his arm.

Clay smiled. Turning his face in the direction of her voice and doffing his hat, he said in a light tone of voice, "Ma'am, I do recollect sayin' I wanted ta let my horse stretch his legs ah mite. And if you recall, the big fella does love ta run."

Victoria stomped her foot and pushed Ramon to the side as she stormed toward the hacienda. As she slammed the door behind her, they heard her yell, "Men! Urrrrr!"

Before either one of them could comment, one of the young boys who worked in the stables came over and took the reins to the three horses.

"Is that you, Felipe?" Clay asked. He knew the big stallion liked Felipe.

"Si, Senor'. It is all right. Midnight and I have become friends. I have been feeding him carrots."

"Midnight?" Clay asked.

"Si, Senor'. That is what I call him because he is Negro – as you say, black like the midnight sky."

Clay smiled and thought that was an ideal name for him. "Ok, Midnight it is."

As Felipe led the horses toward the barn, he crossed his fingers and hoped one day Senor' Brentwood would let him ride the big horse. What a thrill it would be racing across the desert so fast that none of the other horses could keep up with him.

Ramon took Clay by the arm and began leading him to his room. "I think you have caused the Senora to become, how do you say, agitated?"

"Yeah, seems like. There's no figurin' a woman's notions."

"You have that right, my friend. And if you can upset her so easily here at the ranchero, how are you going to deal with her during your long trip to Kansas City and back?"

Before Clay could come up with a retort, Ramon ushered him into his room and turned him so he could sit in the chair next to the patio doors, then disappeared like he hadn't even been there. All Clay heard was the closing of the door.

Clay leaned back and put his hands behind his head, wondering how he was going to convince the Senora she needn't concern herself about going to Kansas City. He would be able to manage by himself.

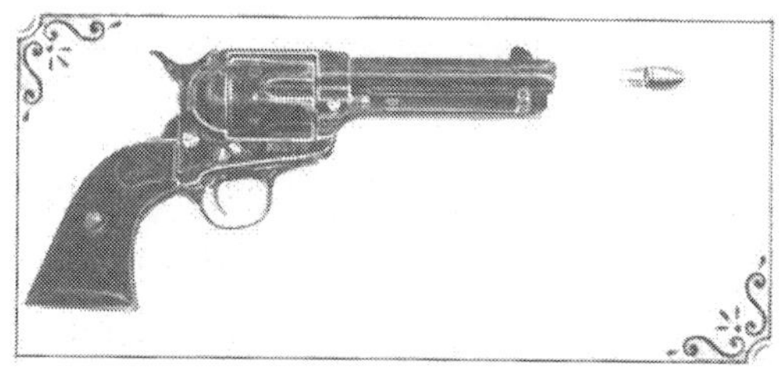

CHAPTER SIXTEEN

-

Clay sat listening to the rumble of the iron wheels rolling down the track. The conductor had informed him they were making good time. He said they had a full load of coal and they were clipping right along at a steady twenty-five miles per hour. “We should be in Wichita shortly,” he said with a grin. “Don’t know what this world is comin’ to. All this new technology is almost more than a body can abide. Heard about a runaway train that got clear up to fifty miles an hour. Couldn’t hardly believe it I’ve known the conductor on that train for years and I know he wouldn’t lie about a thing like that.”

Clay grinned and was about to say something when he smelled a sweet scent. The Senora sat down in the seat next to him and said, "I've brought you a cup of coffee be careful, it's hot."

Taking the cup in both hands, Clay could feel the heat. He was still not sure how his message that he could make this trip alone had not gotten through to her. That had been four days ago.

"We should be in Wichita soon," she said lightly. "You said you want to stay over for a day to take care of some business? What kind of business? Is it something I can help you with?"

Clay sipped the hot coffee, wondering how much about himself he should reveal. He knew he hadn't said anything about having money. If everything was still the same as it was when he left to hunt down Curly and his men, some folks might go so far as to say he was a moderately rich man that wasn't something he went around bragging about. And women being what they were, the Senora would have more questions than a prosecuting attorney at ah murder trial. Evading her question, he said,

"If you can get me to the law office of Fredrick Blackstone, I can handle it from there. Maybe you'd like ta do some shoppin'? When we're both finished, we could go get a couple of rooms and then have ah bite to eat. I heard one of the other passengers saying something about a traveling musical show bein' in town."

"I see," the Senora said, wondering what secrets he was keeping to himself. She looked at his face because of the bandages, she could not read his eyes. Through the window she saw a large herd of cattle with several cowboys riding on both sides and three more cowboys riding drag. The large herd of cattle caused a huge cloud of dust. It reminded her of her of home and her own cattle.

Her silence filled the air and Clay felt he needed to say something else. "He… ah… the attorney, Fredrick Blackstone… he handles a couple of business deals I'm involved in and I just want to check on how they're doin', or not doin'. I haven't been in contact with him for ah couple of years. Shoot, they might have gone belly up for all I know."

Victoria looked over at Clay again and studied him as he sipped his coffee. What wasn't he telling her? There was something he did not want to talk about, of that she was sure what? She wished she could see his eyes. Her female curiosity was building up a good head of steam. She knew so little about him other than Curly and his men had shot him in the head and left him for dead, raped and murdered his wife, stolen his stock and burned his ranch to the ground. Once he recovered from the gunshot wound to his head, he had searched for Curly and his men for two and a half years. When he found them, he avenged the murdering of his wife without a word, and then rode out of town where they met on the road, by her own doing. She had offered him a job and he had taken it.

He knew cattle and men, and was as good a Segundo as she could ask for. He kept himself clean and knew which fork to use at the table. He could even recite poetry. Somewhere in his background, he'd been educated that was about all she knew – not much when it came right down to it. She had hired him based on her instincts and so far they had been correct there was still a lot she didn't know about him and that worried her to distraction. If they were to be married, she…

The train lurched and began to slow down. "Wichita, next stop, in about ten minutes," the conductor called out as he walked through the car. Victoria looked around and saw several people gathering their bags and other belongings.

"There will be a two-hour layover," the conductor said as he left the car to go to the next one and inform the people there.

As Victoria stood up to collect their bags, a porter stopped by and collected the coffee cup from Clay. Clay gave him a dollar. The porter grinned from ear to ear. This was the largest tip he'd ever received. "Anything I can do, sir, you just ask for Henry."

Stepping from the train, they felt the heat and humidity. A thermometer over the door of the station read, 105 degrees.

"Feels and smells about the way I remember it," Clay said as he took her arm, hefting his bag in his other hand.

Wichita was one of the main railheads for cattle drives and several times a year, there would be more than a hundred thousand cattle pass through the famed town Bat Masterson and Wyatt Earp had ruled over. Although there weren't as many shoot- outs as there were a few years ago, men still carried guns to defend themselves.

As they walked down the sidewalk, Victoria was glad Clay had bandages over his eyes and couldn't see what was going on. Almost every man they passed, stopped, eyed her, raised his hat and smiled openly at her.

Not far down the sidewalk, she saw a sign swinging from its hanger that read, Fredrick Blackstone, Attorney at Law.

"His office is just up ahead," she said.

"Good," Clay replied. "I was beginnin' ta think ever man in this town was gonna try and steal you right off my arm."

Her eyes widened with surprise. How did he know that, she wondered?

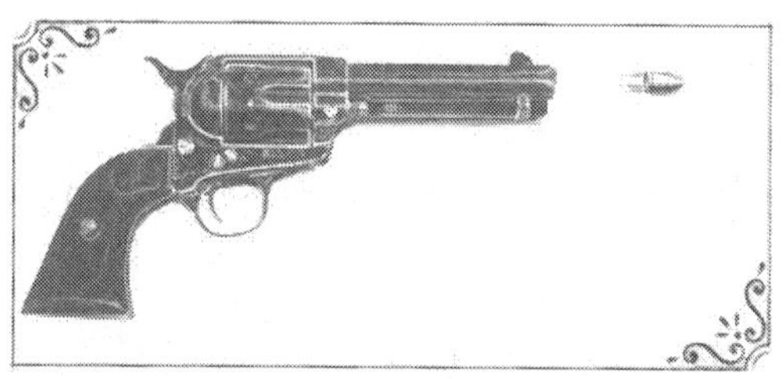

CHAPTER SEVENTEEN

-

At the knock on his office door, Fredrick Blackstone walked over and opened it. Not recognizing the woman, or the man with bandages on his eyes, he asked, "Can I do something for you?" The truth was he was paying more attention to the beautiful woman standing in front of him, looking like a Spanish goddess with her long black hair and dark eyes. Even though the brim of her hat shaded her face, it was not able to hide her beauty, any more than her clothes could hide her superb figure.

Noticing Clay's bandaged face, he said, "If you're looking for the doctor, he's two buildings down on…"

"Mister Blackstone?" Clay asked.

"That would be me," the attorney said, with a questioning look on his face.

Clay turned to the Senora and said, "Thank you. I will meet you here in an hour if that is alright with you?"

"Yes, that will be fine," she said, turning to leave.

Fredrick Blackstone felt a pang of regret watching her walk away. Looking back at the man with the bandaged eyes, he said, "If you don't need the doctor, I'm guessing you think I can be of service to you? Did you have an accident? Are you wanting to sue someone?"

"To begin with, you might want to invite me in, or do you conduct business standin' in your doorway?"

That voice? He knew that voice. No, it couldn't be, he thought. Although?

"Yes, of course, come in. My apologies," he said, taking Clay's arm and leading him to a chair in front of his desk.

After seating himself behind his desk, Fredrick Blackstone asked, "Now, how can I be of service to you, Mister…? He was definitely interested to see if he was correct."

Clay reached into his shirt pocket and took out one of the cigarettes Victoria had rolled for him. Next, he fished in his other shirt pocket, found a match, struck it on his boot and lit the cigarette. After taking a deep puff, he blew the smoke in the air and said, "Brentwood, Clay Brentwood. Last I recall we've known each other for ah spell."

The attorney reached over and took a long, black cigar from a box sitting on his desk and lit it. "I thought your voice sounded familiar it's been awhile, and under all those bandages…" He let the sentence trail off.

Before Clay could respond, the attorney asked, "What happened?"

"Some minor problems during ah fracas between me and some cattle rustlers down in the southern part of the New Mexico Territory. And before you ask, some went ta meet his maker and the rest are in jail down there. They might even have been hung by now. I'm on my way to Kansas City ta see an eye specialist."

"As I recall, you left here trailing the outlaws who murdered your wife," the attorney said, speculatively.

Clay blew more smoke into the air and said, "Let's just say they won't be stealin' any more horses and cattle, or murderin' anymore women."

"I see. And you're on your way somewhere to see about your eyes and since you have to pass through Wichita, you thought you might as well check on your assets. Is that about it?" Fredrick Blackstone was a man who cut to the chase about things.

"That's about the size of it," Clay responded.

The attorney flicked cigar ash into a bucket sitting next to his desk. "You can rest assured they are doing very well. We sold one piece of land to a man and his wife, from Missouri, who came out here wanting to raise wheat. They bought five hundred acres out west of town. They paid cash and you made a tidy sum from the sale. There are still a little over two thousand acres out there for sale, unless you want to save them for yourself?"

Clay thought for a moment and said, "No, sell it. I don't see me comin' back here ta live. If I decide to restock the ranch down in Texas, I'll need money to buy horses and cattle, plus build ah new house, barns, corrals and such."

The attorney smiled and said, "I was wondering if you would be going back?"

"I don't know, yet," Clay said, stubbing out what was left of his cigarette on the sole of his boot. "And the other holdings?" he asked, changing the subject.

"The saloon and hotel are booming because of the cattle drives. The bank is solid, and the other, smaller enterprises, are holding their own. You're a well to do man, Clay Brentwood."

"That's good ta hear," Clay said. "Bein's I'm in good shape financially, I'm thinkin' I might need some money ta pay for the eye doctor up in Kansas City."

"How much do you need? I will make out a withdrawal slip. Do you want bank drafts or cash?"

"I think five thousand in hundred-dollar bank drafts and two thousand in cash will do it. Can I afford that?"

"Consider it done. Do you want it brought here or do you want to go to the bank?"

Clay considered the situation and decided he didn't want to be out in public any more than he had to, not in the condition he was in. He didn't like people starin' at him. "I think it would be best if the money was brought here. And by the way, just how much am I worth, on paper?"

"At the last tally, close to a million dollars," Blackstone said. "Like I said, business has been good and you haven't been around to spend any of it," the attorney said as he laid a piece of paper in front of Clay and placed a pen in his hand, then guided it to the paper. "If you'll just sign here, I'll go to the bank and get it for you."

Clay sat there for a moment, wondering what to do. He had never questioned this man. After all, he had been the attorney of record for both, his wife, and his father-in-law prior to their demises. A million dollars was a lot of money.

After a long pause, the attorney asked, "Would you like to wait and let the young lady witness the transaction? It will make perfect sense if that's what you decide to do; after all, you really don't know me. In fact, I don't think you even know what my fee is for handling your account."

"What is your fee, if I might ask?" Clay said, chuckling.

"Once a year, I take ten percent of the gross, for managing all of the business affairs and making sales of property you want disposed of, which allows me to live quite well. That is the same thing I charged Martha and her father. Actually, you did sign a paper to that affect both, before and after Martha was murdered."

Clay remembered signing some papers while he was recouping at Marion Sooner's ranch in his condition, he would have signed anything.

"No, you can go get the money for me. Put my hand where you want me to sign," Clay said.

When he'd signed the paper, Fredrick Blackstone stood up, blew his breath onto Clay's signature to dry the ink and said, "I'll bring you a cup of coffee to sip on while I'm gone. I'll also bring you a receipt and the young lady can witness it, if you'd like."

"I'd like the receipt I don't need her to witness anything. In fact, the less said about my finances, the better I'll like it."

"I'll consider our dealings as privileged information." And with that, he left the office, leaving Clay with his cup of coffee.

By the time he'd finished the cup of coffee, he began to feel impatient; Fredrick Blackstone should have been back.

Clay stood up, adjusted his jacket and made his way to the door. Outside he tried to remember where the bank was located – just down the street to his right, as he recalled. With great caution, he headed in that direction. He hadn't gone but a few steps when the sound of a young boy drew his attention. "Can I help you mister?"

"I'd be obliged if you could point me in the direction of the bank."

"I'll do better than that," he said as he took Clay by the hand. "I'll walk you to the front door."

Clay felt a little embarrassed, especially when they had gone only ten steps and the boy stopped. "Well, here you are, sir."

Clay reached into his pocket and pulled out what felt like a nickel. "Here you are, son, and thank you very much."

"Gee thanks," the boy said as Clay opened the door and started in.

Clay was half way in the doorway when a gunshot rang out. Automatically, he reached back and shoved the young boy out of the way, just as someone ran into him, trying to get out of the bank in a hurry. What felt like a pistol jammed against his stomach and Clay reacted by instinct.

Clay grabbed the wrist of the hand that held the gun and jerked the man's arm upward. As they both tumbled to the sidewalk, Clay heard the roar of a forty-four pistol going off not too far from his head and at almost the same time, in the near distance he heard someone yell, "Bank Robbery!"

The voice had come from inside the bank and it didn't take Clay more than a heartbeat to realize it was the bank robber he held in his grip. Not being able to see what he was doing, Clay gripped the wrist even tighter and felt the man's grip on the pistol release. At that point, he wrapped his legs around the man's body and hung on.

The man began hitting him on the side of the head with his other fist. Clay could feel the man's head close to his and he reached over and took a bite out of the man's ear. The man screamed and stopped hitting him in the head.

From somewhere, that seemed far away, a voice that sounded like the attorney's said, "It's okay to let go now, Mister Brentwood, we have things under control."

Clay released the man and stood up. He was brushing himself off when Victoria rushed up and said with a chuckle in her voice. "I can't leave you alone for even a minute without you finding some trouble to get into."

Before Clay could say anything, the young boy who had helped him, jumped into the conversation.

"Ya got it wrong, ma'am. This feller here, he ain't in no trouble. He's a hero. He captured the bank robber all by himself, and him blind as ah bat!"

Fredrick Blackstone lifted his hat and addressed the beautiful young woman who had been with Clay, earlier. "We haven't been formally introduced. Fredrick Blackstone, attorney at law. And it's true; Mister Brentwood truly is a hero. He saved the bank a great deal of money."

What the attorney didn't mention was that Clay was also the owner of the bank, and was in fact, saving his own money.

"Enough," Clay said. I just happened to be going into the bank at the same time the bank robber was trying to get out. We bumped into each other - I felt the gun and reacted. That's all. Now can I go into the bank, please?"

As Victoria took his arm to lead Clay into the bank, a large crowd of people who had suddenly gathered around began to applaud.

Clay whispered to Victoria, "Get me into the bank."

As they entered the bank, Victoria said, I am Victoria Marie Christina Claire Ontiveros. Mister Brentwood works for me. He is the Segundo of my ranchero down in the New Mexico territory.

Inside the bank, the attorney leaned over next to Clay and whispered, "What do we do now, about the young lady, I mean?"

Clay sighed, and said, "Senora, there's some things I need to explain. Can we go to the bank president's office?"

After his explanation, the Senora touched his arm and said, "I see. Maybe we should get back on the train as soon as you finish here. We can eat dinner there. If Mister Blackstone can escort you back to the train, I will see you there."

When she turned to leave, all the men stood up and the attorney said, "I will see that he gets there safely."

After she'd gone, Clay felt as though he shouldn't have said anything. For some reason, she was upset and seemed distant.

When his business was finished, he and his attorney went out the back door of the bank, collected Clay's bags, and then made their way to the train.

After saying his goodbyes to the attorney and the bank president, he climbed aboard the train just minutes before the engineer sounded the whistle.

As Fredrick Blackstone watched the train pick up speed, he marveled at Clay Brentwood's luck. Beautiful women seemed to be drawn to the man.

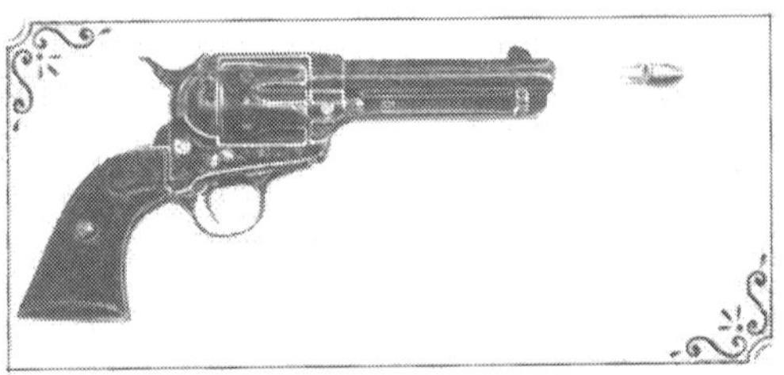

CHAPTER EIGHTEEN

-

Over dinner, Clay tried to explain about how he came to be involved with the attorney, Fredrick Blackstone, and the various investments he came into. He also told her that it was a huge surprise to him that he had that much money.

The Senora was polite and listened and when dinner was over she took his arm and escorted him to his sleeping room. Her touch seemed different and had a bit of a chill to it. At the door, she asked, "Do you need me to pull the bed down for you?"

"No, I'll be alright by myself," Clay answered a bit too quickly.

"Very well then. Thank you for explaining things for me. If you need me, I'll be next door. Otherwise, I'll see you in the morning." And with that, he was standing in the hallway, alone. After only seconds, her door opened and closed. He stood there a moment or two more before entering his own room.

Instead of pulling down his bed, he laid down on the seat and tried to get some rest his mind kept asking him questions he couldn't answer.

Was he wrong to tell the Senora about his investments and his wealth? Why would knowing about it change her opinion of him? Would she still want him as her Segundo now that she knew he was rich? What should he do now? Should he put her on the next train back to Albuquerque? Is that what she would want? There were so many questions and no answers.

It was after midnight before he finally dropped off into a deep sleep.

During the night, there was a brief stop in Topeka, Kansas, which Clay slept through not the Senora. She was still wide awake. She also had questions with no answers - such as, once he got her ranchero up and running, with Ramon trained, would he move on to somewhere else? Would he go back to Texas and rebuild his own ranch? And what about her feelings toward him now that she knew he was rich and didn't need her? Or did he? Had she been wrong to be so cold toward him? How did he feel about her? After all, she was Mexican and he was white. Had her kissing him been too bold on her part? Had she scared him away?

She was sitting on the bench seat, dozing, when a ray of sunlight filled the window next to her face. Trying to come to full wakefulness, she looked around the small room, momentarily confused. She heard the rattle of the train wheels and realized where she was and got quickly to her feet.

After brushing the wrinkles from her skirt, rinsing her face in the bowl of water provided for such, and combing her hair with her fingers, she opened the door and went out into the hallway. At Clay's door, she knocked softly got no answer. She knocked again, louder this time. And when she still got no answer, she tried the knob and opened the door. The room was empty.

Turning, she hurried into the passenger car and looked around. Several people looked up at her none of them was Clay. She made her way to the dining car and saw him sitting in a chair, eating breakfast. Henry was pouring coffee into Clay's cup. Henry looked up and smiled, then said something to Clay.

Clay stood up and faced in her direction. "Good mornin', sleepyhead. Are you ready for some breakfast? Henry said we should be in Kansas City shortly."

Henry pulled out a chair for Victoria and she sat down.

"Coffee or tea, ma'am?"

"Tea, and something light to eat. I'll leave it up to you," Victoria said with a smile.

Clay sat down and said, "I'm…"

Before he could go any further, Victoria reached across and laid her hand on his and said, "Please, you do not have to explain anything. It is I who should apologize for being so rude. It is none of my business how much money you have or do not have. The fact that you are a very wealthy man was a bit of a shock at first - that is all. You have not talked much about your past; about having money or much of anything about yourself, and the truth is, it is none of my business. You agreed to be my Segundo and help put my ranchero back on its feet, which you have done quite well. I do not have the right to ask for more."

Henry appeared with the Senora's tea and a piece of pastry.

The Senora started to pay him Henry said, "Oh no, ma'am, Mister Brentwood has already taken care of everything – and right nicely at that."

Henry gave them a big smile and said, "Y'all eat up now; we be pullin' into the station directly."

After Henry had gone, Victoria said, "Thank you for breakfast."

Clay took a cigarette from his shirt pocket and raised it, asking, "Will it bother you if I smoke while you eat?"

Victoria smiled and said, "Please, go ahead. My father used to like having a cigar after his meals."

Clay lit his cigarette and took a puff, then said, "Look, I'm not much on dancin' around a subject, so I'll just say what's on my mind."

After a moment, he said, "I don't know why I haven't said much about myself other than I didn't feel like my past was of much importance. Like you said, you hired me ta put your ranch back in shape and that's what I've been tryin' ta do. And if I might say so, I agree with you, it's comin' along nicely. I'm of the mind that our relationship has become ah mite more than boss and foreman I'm not real sure what that means. I'm not real good at figurin' out how women think." At that, he took a moment and when she didn't say anything, he went on.

"I don't know, maybe you'd feel more comfortable catching the next train back west. If that's what you'd like ta do, I'm sure I'll be able to get along. Henry said he has a cousin in Kansas City who can help me find where I need ta go."

After a long silence, Victoria wiped her lips with the napkin Henry had left with her pastry, and asked, "Is that what you want, for me to go home and stay out of your way?"

Clay coughed on the cigarette smoke caught in his throat. Now why would she say something like that? Hell, he hadn't wanted her ta come along in the first place she had come anyway, and he had to admit, so far, it had been nice having her along. And now, he had gone and hurt her feelings. One side of him wanted her to stay and the other side wanted her to go.

"Victoria," he said, trying to put her at ease. "I just want you ta do what makes you the most comfortable."

About then, the train began slowing down and the conductor came through the car, calling out, "Kansas City, Kansas. Kansas City, Kansas. One-hour stop, then on to Kansas City, Missouri, and Saint Louis, Missouri."

Without saying anything, Victoria stood up and took Clay's arm. "We'd better get our bags; the train will be pulling into the station in just a few minutes."

Victoria saw Henry and waved to him, and after a generous tip, Henry carried their bags while Victoria escorted Clay off the train.

As they stepped off the train, Clay once again realized he had absolutely no idea about how to deal with women. With Martha it had been easy; she ran the house and he ran the ranch. And if he needed someone to bounce ideas off of, she was always there. She was his wife and partner. Victoria had her own ranch and he was just an employee. Well, maybe not just an employee that was still a question that hadn't been properly addressed.

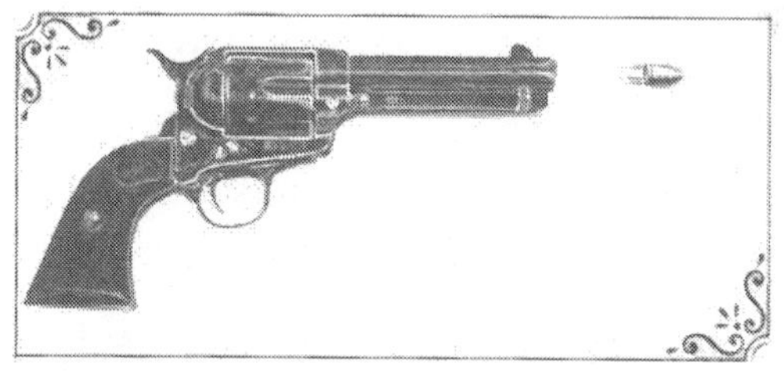

CHAPTER NINETEEN

The train station was the largest building Victoria had ever seen and she marveled at the amount of people coming and going. With a bit of sadness, she wondered whether someday, Albuquerque or Santa Fe would grow to be this big and overcrowded? She hoped not. She liked both towns the way they were.

After one of the porters told them the Kansas City Hotel was just down the street a block and a half, they decided to walk. She thought it would be good to stretch their legs, along with getting a look at the famous city.

The air smelled of coal smoke and cattle, a strange combination Victoria thought as they walked along. She also read the giant signs on the fronts of buildings as they passed by.

Crackers and Confectionery Company – The home of - Krispy Crackers, Hi Ho Crackers and Hydrox Cookies.

Another sign read – John Taylor Dry Goods Company – We carry a full line of Corsets, Bustles and Ladies Underwear. Our Specialty – Ladies genuine Alaska Down Bustles.

This one she snickered at, under her breath.

Because of the train station and the stockyards, the Kansas City Hotel was kept well supplied with customers. At the desk, she told the man behind the counter their names and reminded him they had telegraphed ahead for reservations.

He smiled and rang a bell.

Clay signed in and paid for both rooms. A man in his fifties carried their bags to their respective rooms.

At the door to her room, Victoria informed Clay that she would like to take a bath and put on fresh clothes before they went to see the eye doctor – and suggested he do the same.

The porter suggested the bathing rooms down the hall and said he would reserve one for each of them. He also informed Clay that he would be happy to escort him to the bathing room and back.

Inside his room, Clay took off the bandages and then opened his eyes slowly. Everything was a bit blurry he could make things out if he concentrated. He wasn't totally blind, which gave him hope.

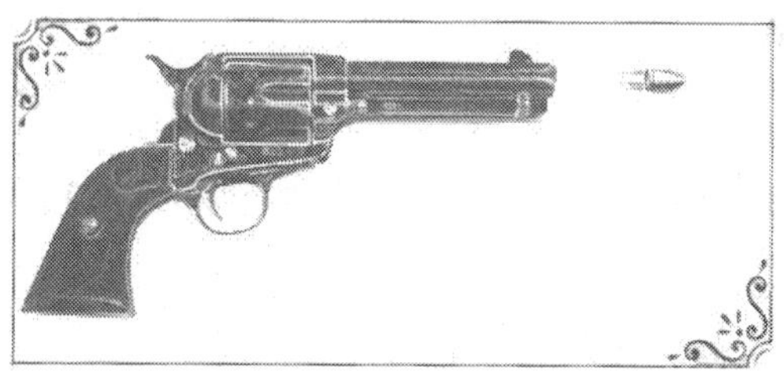

CHAPTER TWENTY

The doctor's office was about a mile from the hotel. The carriage driver informed them he had delivered people here before and told them the office was on the second floor.

They found the door with a sign on the front that read, Doctor Alfred Trails, Eye Specialist.

A frail young man in his late twenties, sporting a goatee and mustache, with an uncontrolled mat of hair, opened the door and ushered them in. Victoria smiled inwardly, realizing the young man was trying to make himself look older, hoping his clients would believe him to be more experienced than he was.

The examination took more than an hour. Clay was seated in a special chair and the doctor attached an apparatus to Clay's head that held his eyelids open while the doctor shined a light in his eyes and looked deep into them through a magnifying glass attached to his own head.

He studied each eye with great care, making notes and a lot of hum, ah-hum sounds that frustrated Clay he held his tongue.

Victoria watched with great interest. This young man was like no doctor she had ever seen before and she was impressed. He was professional and quite thorough with his examination.

Before the examination began, he had explained in detail, that he had studied in Germany under the great Herman Von Helmhotz, inventor of the ophthalmoscope – the very device he would be using today to examine Clay's eyes.

When he finished the examination, he went to his desk and wrote more notes. When he'd finished he went to a cupboard and got a bottle of something, then explained there were still a few small pieces of rock embedded in Clay's eyes that would need to be removed.

"If not removed, those small pieces of splintered rock will never allow the eyes to heal. Once they're gone, I believe your eyes will heal nicely, Mister Brentwood. Would you like me to do that today? The price will be twelve dollars."

"Do what you need to do, son," Clay replied. He wanted his sight back.

First, the doctor gave Clay a teaspoon of Laudanum that he explained would allow Clay to relax during the operation. After a few minutes, he leaned Clay back on the chair and carefully put drops into Clay's eyes that stung somewhat not so bad that Clay couldn't stand it. The laudanum was working.

"How do you feel, Mister Brentwood?" the doctor asked.

"Like I've had too much redeye," Clay answered.

The doctor looked over at Victoria and smiled.

"That's fine, Mister Brentwood. Now, please try to hold as still as possible, this is a very delicate operation."

Victoria watched with amazement as the doctor removed nine very small pieces of rock slivers from Clay's eyes and put them in a pan – four from one eye and five from the other.

When he could find no more slivers, he put some different drops in Clay's eyes and to Clay's dismay, bandaged them again.

"You will need to come back every day for the next several days so I can examine your eyes and put in more medicine, if needed. Within a week your eyesight should almost be as good as it was before. It will take several weeks before they are restored fully," the doctor told Clay as he finished putting the bandages on his eyes.

Clay reached into his pocket and pulled out a wad of bills and held them out.

"Victoria, would you pay the man, please?"

She took the money and counted out twelve dollars, then placed the rest back on Clay's hand.

"What time tomorrow?" Victoria asked.

"Let's say, around two. Is that convenient for you?"

"Yes, two will be fine. And thank you doctor," Victoria said as she took Clay's arm and escorted him toward the door.

"By the way, Mister Brentwood," the doctor asked as Victoria was opening the door, "how did you get all those pieces of rock in your eyes?"

"Bullet ricocheted off a boulder near my head," Clay called over his shoulder as they walked out into the hallway.

As the door was closing, Victoria glanced over her shoulder and saw the look of shock on the doctor's face, as he stood there with his mouth hanging open.

During the following week, they went to the doctor every day and every day the doctor hummed and uh-hummed – put more medicine in Clay's eyes and put on fresh bandages.

Every evening they rode the cable cars and visited all the sights Kansas City had to offer. They ate in fine restaurants and went to shows. Victoria would explain what was going on and Clay would listen to the songs. She even bought some new clothes.

On the seventh day, after a thorough examination and having Clay read a chart hanging on the doctor's wall, he declared Clay fit and gave him a bottle of eye drops to put in his eyes at bedtime.

To the young doctor's surprise, Clay left another one hundred dollars on his desk, and then thanked him again by pumping the doctor's hand up and down until he thought it might come loose from his arm. He'd had happy patients before none as exuberant as this one, or as free with his money.

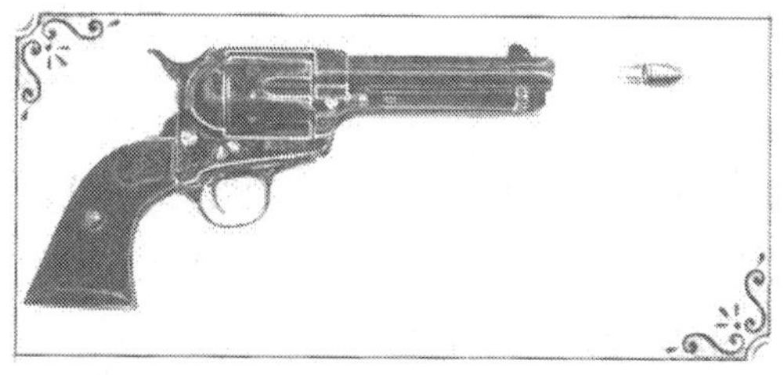

CHAPTER TWENTY-ONE

The Senora noticed Clay's head leaning back and his mouth open as she came to get him for lunch in the dining car. Rather than touching him she called out to him. "Clay, it's time for lunch."

Clay raised his head, rubbed his eyes and said, "The sound those wheels are making was about to put me to sleep."

"Yes, I could tell how close you were by the deep snoring coming from your seat," she teased.

A bit embarrassed, Clay stood up and followed Victoria to the dining car where they had lunch and talked about the ranchero and wondered how Ramon was handling things.

So far, the return trip had been pretty boring. They spent two days in Wichita where Clay took ten thousand dollars in bank drafts from one of his accounts to add to the money he already had on him.

"Never know when ah man might need some money," he told Victoria as he tucked five hundred in cash in his front pocket.

She smiled and nodded her head said nothing – there was apprehension showing in her eyes. Clay noticed kept it to himself.

Clay excused himself and went into the bank president's office and put the rest of the money into a money belt he'd purchased in Kansas City, strapped it around his waist and then tucked in his shirt to hide the money belt.

At Fredrick Blackstone's office, the attorney informed them that everything was running smoothly, and inquired about the operation to Clay's eyes.

"Smooth as honey on ah hot rock," Clay told him. "The doctor was young he sure knew his stuff – removed nine more pieces of rock slivers. Studied in Germany he said. And the price the young feller charged was so small, I felt guilty and gave him a bit more than he asked for," Clay said, seeing Victoria smile and nod her head.

They had talked about that after leaving the doctor's office, and she had agreed it had been the right thing to do. "After all, how much is a person's eyesight worth?" she asked.

"I reckon I got off pretty cheap at that," Clay agreed.

The attorney sat down at his desk and took a pen from the ink well.

"I'm very glad the operation was successful. Now, if you would leave his name and address with me before you go – I'd like to have it on hand just in case I run onto someone who might need his services. Good eye doctors are few and far between."

After Clay and Victoria left his office, Fredrick Blackstone looked at the name and address Clay had given him. "Maybe I'll take a trip up to Kansas City," he said, lighting a cigar and leaning back in his chair.

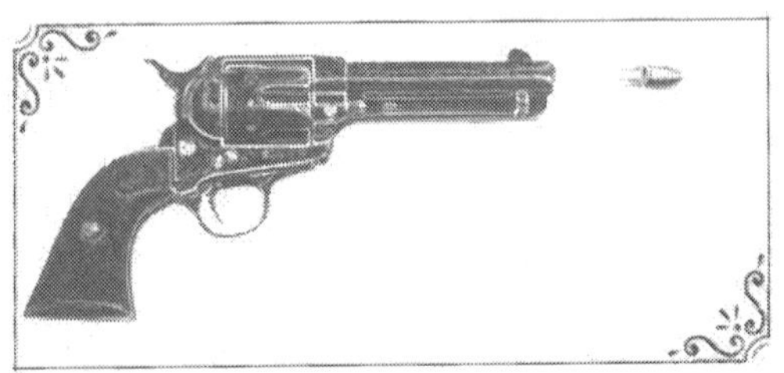

CHAPTER TWENTY-TWO

-

At the train station, after welcoming them home, Jose Garcia loaded their bags into the wagon and together, with the Senora and Clay, they headed for the ranchero.

"And how are things going at the ranchero, Jose?" Victoria inquired.

"Not so good," Jose said with the hunch of his shoulders.

"Is Ramon having problems?" Clay asked.

"Si, Senor'," he said, tapping the reins lightly on the horse's hindquarters.

After more than a minute's silence, Victoria could stand it no longer and asked, "Well, are you going to tell us what is wrong, or are we to suffer in silence?"

Allowing the horses to continue down the road at their own pace, he swept off his sombrero and turned in his seat and looked directly at the Senora. "It is the slavers, they have returned. They have taken several young women. Manuel Rodriguez and Juan Corrales were shot down when they tried to resist. I am sorry to tell you of this trouble, Senora you asked me to tell you."

Victoria sighed and said, "You did the right thing, Jose. And what of Ramon?"

"He took four Vaqueros with him to try to get the women back on the second day, he was shot in the leg and they brought him back. The doctor said he will live for now he can only hobble around.

"Slavers?" Clay asked. "I thought that was stopped years ago."

"For the Yankees, maybe for us, being so close to the border; from time to time they raid us and take our women and young girls. They are never seen or heard from again. This is the second time they have raided in this area. Our hearts are sad.

The last time, they raided not only our ranchero also several other rancheros, along with taking several of the young women from the town.

"It is said they take them to Mexico City and sell the older ones to the highest bidder, where they spend the rest of their lives working the fields. The pretty young girls are sold into prostitution."

Clay looked around and saw they were not far from the ranchero. He would get some supplies and head out at first light. In fact, he was so deep in thought, he was slow to react when he saw Jose driven from the seat and heard the sound of the rifle. When he reached for his pistol, he realized he didn't have it on – he had left it at the ranchero.

Standing up to climb into the empty space left by Jose and take the reins of the runaway horses, he felt a bullet slam into his left side and heard the roar of the rifle as he felt himself being pushed out of the wagon by the force of the bullet. He landed face down in the ditch with a sharp pain where the bullet had struck him. Being gut shot was no way to die, Clay thought. Especially, just after getting his eyesight back. Just before things began to fade he heard the voice of Harley Grimm.

"Got ya right in the gut, Mister Segundo - Jest like I wanted to. You'll suffer this day before ya die. I tole ya I would get even." And with that, Harley Grimm leaned his head back and laughed with one of those snorting kinds of laughs.

As things began to go black, Clay heard a man with a Mexican accent say, "You were right my friend. The Senora will bring mucho dinero down in Mexico City."

The last thing Clay heard was the sound of hooves as Harley and his friend started down the road in pursuit of the Senora who had climbed into the seat and taken up the reins. She figured Clay was dead and she wasn't about to get captured without a fight. If she could outrun them and get to the ranchero…

"She is purty, jest like I said," Harley yelled as they raced down the road. "Yep, she'll fetch us ah right nice price, alright."

After chasing the wagon for nearly a half a mile, they caught up with the Senora.

Harley's friend, a tall Mexican man in his forties, with a drooping mustache and a scar across his nose and down to the right side of his mouth, rode up alongside the lead horse, grabbed the reins and pulled the horses to a halt.

Harley pulled his pistol and pointed it at the Senora. "Lady, I don't relish shootin' you cause that would cost us ah lot of money if'n you don't come peaceful-like, that's exactly what I'm gonna do."

The Senora knew when she had lost and held out her hands so Harley could tie them together, and then he tied her to the seat.

"You reckon we could have ah little fun before we take her ta Mexico?" Harley asked.

"My friend, I am afraid I have some very bad news for you. I have made a slight change in our arrangement."

"But I reckoned we would share fifty-fifty," Harley said, a bit confused.

"I have decided I do not want to share her, or the money." And with that, he raised his pistol and shot Harley right in the middle of his gut.

Harley grabbed the saddle horn and somehow stayed in the saddle. The tall Mexican rode over next to Harley and kicked him in the side, which caused Harley to leave his saddle and fall into the back of the wagon, where he landed hard against the seat.

The tall Mexican then took the reins of the team and turned the wagon around and led them back down the road to where Clay still lay, face down in the ditch. After stopping the horses, he dragged Harley from the wagon and gave him a shove.

Harley landed in the ditch not four feet from where Clay lay, quiet and still.

The sky was filled with stars and the temperature had dropped when Clay felt himself shudder and opened his eyes. He lay there for several minutes, feeling the pain in his stomach before he rolled over onto his back and placed his hand over the spot where the bullet had struck him.

He was surprised when he felt no blood. Next, he probed the hole in his shirt and gave a laugh and lurched when he heard Harley's voice.

"What are you laughin' about, Segundo, you gonna die just like me."

"Afraid not, Harley, the jokes on you."

"What'ya mean by that?" Harley asked, obviously in pain.

"You killed my money belt," Clay replied.

"I killed what?"

"When you shot me, your bullet hit my money belt, which has a lot of money in it and the bullet is lodged in the money. If it's any consolation for ya," Clay said, matter of factually, "I do have ah sore stomach."

"You no good son of…" and with that Harley took a last gasp and his eyes went blank.

Clay rolled over and slowly got to his feet. Standing there in the road, he dug out the piece of lead and held it up in the moonlight. As he stood there, staring at the piece of lead that was meant for his death, a thought came to him. What if he had been still blind? "Man doesn't take enough time to think about things," he said to the cold wind that was blowing across the desert. "I reckon he should take more notice of things like, seein', hearin', feelin', and such," knowin' he would appreciate them ah bit more from now on.

After putting the bullet in his pocket as a reminder to how close he had come to dying, Clay turned and headed for the ranchero.

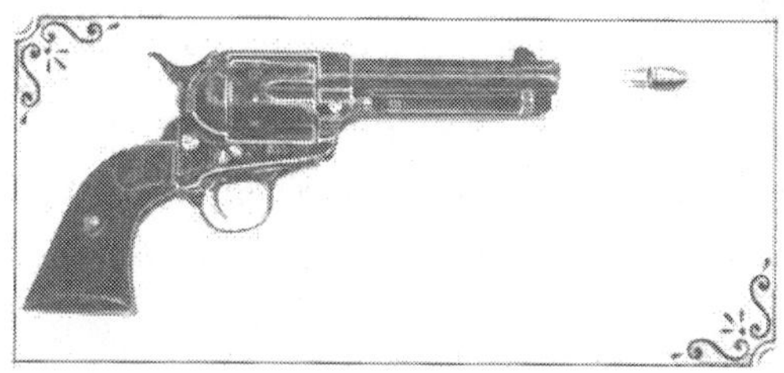

CHAPTER TWENTY-THREE

The sun was up and the men were going about their daily routines when Clay stumbled in through the front gate of the hacienda. The first to notice him was Felipe, the stable boy. "Senor' Clay!" he yelled as he ran over and took Clay's arm and helped him to the bench next to the well. One of the older women was already there with a dipper of cold water.

After two dippers of water, Clay explained to the people still left at the hacienda what had happened and what he planned to do; then asked for as many details as they could remember.

After thirty minutes of listening, Clay still didn't know much more than he already knew and was about to go to his room to check on his aching stomach, when Anna appeared and told him she had breakfast waiting for him.

After a breakfast of eggs, beans, bacon, and tortillas, Clay topped it off with two cups of coffee. He was about to ask if there was enough hot water so he might take a bath, when Anna handed him a towel and said, "Maybe you would like to have a bath and some clean clothes, Senor', before you go after the Senora?"

Clay grinned and stood up, taking the towel from Anna. "You took the words right out of my mouth."

Back in his room, bathed and dressed in clean clothes, he checked the large purple-blue-black splotch of skin on his stomach. It was still tender didn't look much worse than a nasty bruise. Some of the money on the other hand, didn't fare so well. Almost half of it had a large hole through the middle – a cheap price for saving his life, he figured. He was about to button his shirt when there came a knock at the door and as he turned, it opened.

Without a word, Anna came in, pushed his shirt aside and gently rubbed some liniment on his bruised stomach; and then wrapped his waist with a piece of cloth.

Turning for the door she called over her shoulder, "It is aloe I put on you. It will help heal your wound and make riding easier. I have a packet of food for you to take and Pablo is making packs of food for your horses. Find her and bring her home, Senor' Clay; along with the others, if you can."

And with that she was gone. Clay just stood there wondering about women. They were plumb a mystery.

When Clay got out to the barn, Felipe and Pablo had already gotten his animals ready. The black stallion was saddled. A lop-eared mule was loaded with food and two bags of water for him and the horses, along with the other things he would need for the trip. There was also an extra mount, a high-spirited steel-dust that only a strong rider could control, allowing Clay to switch horses from time to time – giving the black stallion a rest.

After looking over the steel-dust, Clay grinned and said, "You didn't happen ta load any extra ammo, did ya?" Clay asked.

"Si, Senor' - one hundred rounds," Pablo said, grinning from ear to ear, pointing to the saddlebags on the pack mule.

"Let's hope I don't have ta use them," Clay said.

Before mounting the black stallion, Clay ruffled Felipe's hair and said, "You keep an eye on things while I'm gone."

"Si, Senor'," Felipe said, grinning like he'd just been given an important job.

As Clay rode through the gates, Anna and all the others stood watching him go; hope in their eyes and making the sign of the cross for his protection.

Looking across the barren land where the desert winds can destroy tracks in a matter of minutes, Clay shook his head. Mexico City was a long way off and it would be difficult to hide them all. Finding them would be the hard part.

Heading southeast, it took Clay three days before he stumbled onto what looked like deep wagon tracks such as the kidnappers would use to transport their human prey.

From the description the people at the hacienda had given him, the wagon had to be one similar to the ones law officials transported criminals in, which meant it would be heavy and they couldn't travel as fast as he could. He just hoped the tracks would not disappear, altogether. At least he knew their destination, or assumed he did.

That night he found where they had camped and he was sure he spotted a boot print similar to the boots the Senora wore. It wasn't positive evidence but it was, at least, something to go on.

The area wasn't much there among the Gypsum boulders that were worn by the dry winds of time was a small pool of water. The pool seemed to be kept full from some unseen source. It was small and almost hidden among the rocks, which made it hard to get to, forcing him to water the horses one at a time.

When he'd removed the burdens from their backs, he rubbed them down and tethered them so they could find what little grass that was available, which wasn't much. The kidnapper's horses had fed here just a few days ago and there wasn't much in the way of grass left. The donkey found some pigweed and was making due with that, along with a little grain he fed them while water boiled for coffee and beans and bacon cooked over a small fire.

After supper, Clay scouted around in the waning light still left to him before night fell. Near where the rear of the wagon would have been, he found an earring that he recognized as being one of the Senora's. Was she leaving a marker, hopefully to be followed? Or did she just lose it, he wondered?

The next morning, Clay was on the move by the time the sun was creeping over the horizon; and by mid-morning he had put close to ten miles behind him. The deep-set wagon tracks with at least six riders flanking each side made the trail easy to follow and he was making good time. He was riding the steel-dust, who seemed to be bursting with energy and wanted to run Clay held him to a steady lope so he could keep sight of the wagon tracks. He was making good time, when suddenly the wind began to pick up and black clouds came rolling across the sky like a herd of buffalo. Along with lightning, the sound of thunder rumbled inside the ominous looking clouds.

Instantly, Clay scanned the horizon, looking for a place to get in out of the approaching storm, which looked to be a mean one didn't see any such refuge.

Glancing down at the desert, his eyes took a double take; the tracks were gone!

Circling around he saw the tracks had suddenly made a turn toward the east, right out here in the middle of no man's land, with no land marks to guide them. Now, why had they decided to make a turn right here at this particular spot?

He had no answer knew he had no choice but to follow them. Within a mile, he felt the first drops of rain, driven by the heavy winds, smashing into his back.

For the next hour and a half, Clay could do nothing but endure the fierceness of the storm. The black clouds had obliterated the sun. Being able to follow the wagon tracks in darkness as black as a night with no stars, was impossible. With his head bowed, he rode on, in what he hoped was an easterly direction.

When finally the storm had passed, it ended almost as abruptly as it had started. Clay hauled up the steel-dust and watched as the storm moved on across the wide sky with its driving wind and pounding rain.

Looking down, he wasn't surprised to see the land absent of any wagon tracks. Either he was off the trail, or the storm had wiped out any chance he had of following the kidnappers. He zigzagged back and forth to a distance of half a mile on either side of his line of travel, looking for their tracks.

He was about to give up, telling himself he had been wasting precious time, when all of a sudden there they were – the imprints of four wagon wheels where they had stopped and the weight had been enough to not be washed away by the storm he saw no evidence of them having camped here.

"Now why would they stop the wagon out here in the middle of the desert without makin' camp?" he asked the steel dust, who just raised his ears, and snorted, impatient to be on his way.

Clay was about to move on when he saw a sparkle in the sunlight. Getting down he brushed away sand from the mate to the earring he carried in his pocket. Whistling, he looked up at the steel-dust and said, "Would you look at what I found? There's no doubt about it, the lady is leaving a trail. Thank you, Senora."

The steel-dust pawed the ground as if answering him.

Clay got a concerned look on his face. "How would she know I was coming after her? She saw me get shot, so she must think I'm dead," he said to the horses.

The black stallion shook his head while the other two just looked at him with blank stares.

Clay stood, looking around. As far as he could see in any direction, there was nothing but desert surrounding small mesas, here and there. He could see how easy it would be for a man to get lost out here. Everything looked the same; at least to the untrained eye. The Indian was born and raised here, and by the time he reached young manhood, he knew every inch of the desert – knew where the waterholes were, knew where the salt flats spread themselves across the desert floor. He even knew what was edible and what was not.

Only the white man would come here in his search for gold, silver or treasure on a map purchased in a saloon - unprepared - wandering around in circles before he died of thirst and famine just yards, sometimes feet, from both - if the Indians didn't kill him first.

Clay Brentwood did not claim to know the country like the Indians did during the past two and a half years, he'd learned a thing or two about survival - things he hoped would serve him now. Stepping back into the saddle, he headed southeast, following the trail of the slavers as best as he could, hoping he would catch up to them before the women were sold into slavery.

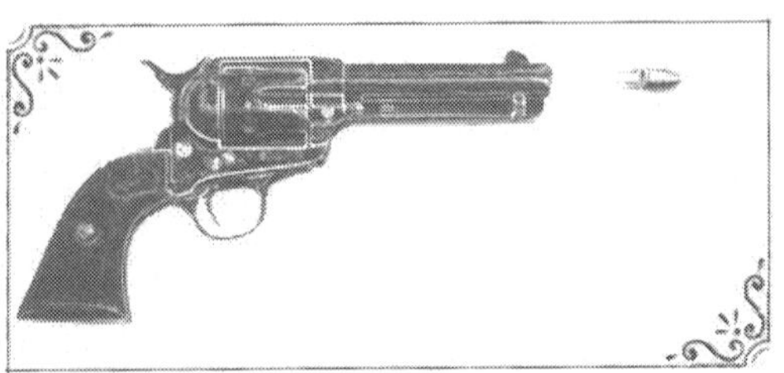

CHAPTER TWENTY-FOUR

-

Three days later, Clay felt like he was close to becoming a statistic – one of the stupid white men who died wandering around in territory he knew so little about. After nineteen days following hit and miss tracks across the windblown desert, and suffering through blistering heat and torrential rain storms, he was tired clear down to the marrow of his bones and still no idea whether or not he was close to catching up with the slavers.

Even though he was used to spending long days in the saddle during the time he had been tracking the Beeler gang, this time it was different. He didn't have the luxury of stopping whenever he felt like it - most of the time he was in the saddle from sunup until sundown, except for short breaks to rest the horses.

During this entire trip, most of the watering holes he'd found so far barely had enough water for the horses to have a drink, with a little for him to wet his tongue and throat. Twice, after two more hard rainstorms, he had found pools of water enough to replenish his water bags. The wind and boiling sun made him pay the price for invading this part of the country. If it was so hard for him, what was it like for the slavers and the women?

Clay Brentwood was tired, hungry and frustrated. He hadn't had a bath or shaved since he'd left the hacienda. He was out of food except for a small amount of coffee and a few pieces of jerky. There hadn't been any water for him or the animals for the past two days and both, he and the horses were struggling. If he didn't find water and maybe some game to eat and grass for the animals soon, they would all die out here in this God forsaken, barren land, and wind up as food for the buzzards and coyotes. The only thing that kept him going on was the thought of what the Senora and the other women must be going through. If he didn't find them and get them back, who would?

The big stallion came to a halt, causing Clay to jerk himself awake, draw his pistol and look around. Apparently, he had fallen asleep in the saddle and now sat staring at a mountain looming in front of him. Dropping his eyes toward the ground he saw a clear set of wagon tracks leading up the trail. When he realized he'd drawn his pistol, he dropped it back into his holster, feeling a little bit embarrassed.

Just ahead, not more than a few hundred feet, was a few trees and a patch of grass. He eased the horses and pack mule forward until they reached the shelter of the trees. Once there, he stepped down and released the cinches on the saddles to allow the animals to at least get something in their bellies. There was no water that he could see at least there was some shade, the first he'd had in some time.

Clay sat down and leaned his back against a tree, enjoying the shade. He ate a piece of jerky while the horses and the mule fed on a small patch of grass.

When he'd finished the piece of jerky, he rolled a smoke. The smoke felt raw against his dry throat maybe it would help stave off the hunger and thirst that he felt.

As he sat there, he wondered how the women were doing? Scared, no doubt about that - and probably wondering if anyone would be coming to get them and take them home? Of course, the Senora would assure them that someone would be coming.

Now all he had to do would be to survive long enough to find them, and then figure out how to rescue them from at least a dozen hard cases who would try to shoot him first.

He finished his cigarette and snuffed it out on the heel of his boot, tore up the paper and spread it out, letting the wind scatter it across the land. The trees in this area were long in need of water and he didn't want to start a fire.

After tightening the cinches, Clay stepped into the saddle and headed up the steep mountain trail. The going was slow and Clay took his time, not pushing the horses or the mule. After half an hour, he stopped and let the horses and the mule take another breather.

Looking back down the trail, Clay wondered how the animals pulling the slave wagon had fared. He didn't know whether horses or mules were pulling the wagon, or maybe even oxen; but no matter, the trail was steep and according to the depth of the tracks, the slave wagon was heavy. Going would be slow.

After ten minutes, Clay set out again. He didn't want to wear out his animals on the other hand he didn't want to waste the day lounging around. He needed to get on the downside part of this mountain.

It was late afternoon when he topped over the rise and looked down the backside of the mountain. As he sat looking out over the vastness of the land, Clay guessed he had climbed to somewhere in the neighborhood five thousand feet. Not far below him and to the left, where the trail led, he was surprised to see the lights of a town. Thoughts of food, water and a soft bed, urged him on down the trail. He would need to keep his eyes open for the prison wagon.

As he neared the edge of the small community, he stopped and read the sign.

WELCOME TO ANTELOPE WELLS

POPULATION, 124

ELEVATION 4665 FEET

GO SOUTH OF TOWN AND YOU'RE IN MEXICO

Clay grinned and lightly tapped the steel-dust in the ribs with the heels of his boots. The steel-dust, tired from the climb up the mountain, lifted his head and headed into town, hoping for some rest and something to eat.

As Clay rode through the small town, it looked clean and fairly quiet for a border town. At the livery stable, a man with a mat of coal black hair, who Clay guessed to be around forty, greeted Clay. He was long and lean, six feet or more and skinny, and his deep suntan made him look almost as dark as a Mexican.

"Howdy, stranger. You look like you've come ah fair piece," he said with a grin. "And yer animals look plumb tuckered out. If'n yer lookin' ta put'em up fer the night, I'll treat'um real good; give'um ah rub down, oats and fresh cut hay fer four bits apiece and if'n yer hungry we got us ah good café jest up the street, if'n yer partial ta Mexican food, that is. And if you need a place ta hunker down fer the night, you can sleep here in the barn or over to the hotel which is run by ah friend of mine, Brady Hooks. You jest tell'm Nathan sent ya."

Clay marveled at the amount of information the man could spout out without stopping for a breath.

"Well now, that all sounds mighty nice to me," Clay said as he stepped down and reached into his pocket and pulled out two dollars in silver and handed to the man. "And if you do a good job, the extra four bits is for you."

Nathan's eyes lit up and his grin told Clay all he needed to know.

"Yes sir! They'll get the best care they ever had! You can count on thet."

Clay thought back to Jose as he eyed the man and said, "Go slow and easy with the black. He was a wild stallion not too far back, and he's just now letting strangers do for him."

Nathan walked over to the black stallion and gently rubbed his nose and spoke softly, offering him a small amount of sugar. "We're gonna be good friends big fella. You jest let ole Nathan do for you and you won't regret it."

The black stallion rolled his eyes and curled his lips, ready to bite the man's hand his soft words, gentle touch, and the sweet taste of sugar, for some reason made the big stallion feel comfortable and he decided to trust this man, as he licked the last of the sugar from the liveryman's hand.

Clay asked Nathan if he'd seen a group of men with a prisoner wagon loaded with women come through town.

Nathan shook his head and said, "Sorry I've been gone fer the past week – jest got back last night and the Mexican feller who was takin' care of the place for me went back down ta Mexico. I'm sure Lopez; the bartender can help you out. He knows purt-near everthin' that goes on around here."

Clay walked up the street with his saddlebags slung over his shoulder, knowing the animals would be well taken care of. Now he would do for himself. He would rent a room, get a bath, a shave and get into some clean clothes before he stopped at the saloon for a drink and find out what kind of information Lopez might have. If there was any news of the slave wagon, the saloon would be the place to get it. Bartenders always seemed to know everything that went on in town. And, after that, he would fill his belly with food somebody else had cooked. Mexican food would do just fine. Since working for the Senora, he'd taken a liking to Mexican food.

As he stepped up onto the wooden sidewalk in front of the only hotel in town, he heard the roll of thunder. Clay turned his head toward the sound and saw black clouds rolling across the late afternoon sky. The heavy rain had not quite reached the town but it was on its way.

Normally, Clay didn't mind sleeping out under the stars tonight there would be no stars, just pounding rain and he'd had enough of that, lately.

He was looking forward to sleeping in a soft bed. And knowing the horses and the mule would be inside where it was dry and would be taken care of, gave Clay piece of mind. After all, if a man didn't take care of his horses, he just might find himself afoot out in the middle of nowhere. Only a tenderfoot would do something stupid like that, or maybe an Indian who was being chased. Then he would ride the animal to death, then eat him.

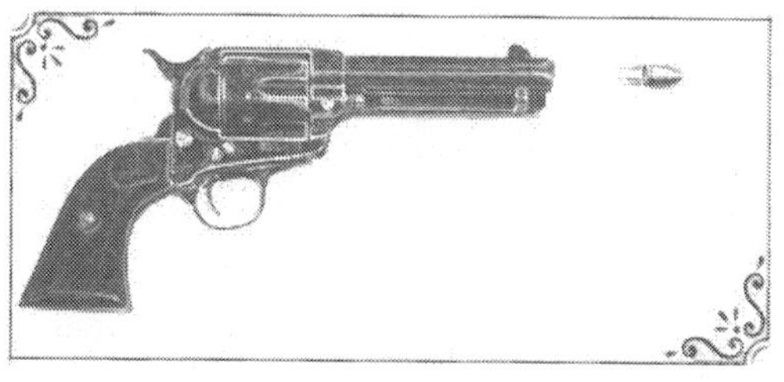

CHAPTER TWENTY-FIVE

-

The hotel was clean and well furnished with a mix of American and Mexican furniture. Behind the check-in counter, Brady Hooks, a balding man in his late forties was leaning back in a chair, eyes closed and snoring loudly. A book was lying on his belly paunch. Brady was only bald on top. The sides and back of his head was covered with slightly graying hair that hung to his shoulders. His light gray shirt was clean a bit frayed. The suspenders that normally held up his gabardine pants had slipped off his shoulders and hung loosely against his arms.

Clay tapped the bell sitting on the counter and Brady jerked awake, causing the chair to upset and Brady going one way, the book and chair going the other.

Embarrassed, Brady jumped to his feet and adjusted his suspenders back onto his shoulders. “Good afternoon,” he said. “Looking for a room?”

“No, I just came inside to get out of the weather,” Clay was tempted to say , instead, he said, “Yes, if you have one available.”

“I’m sure we can accommodate you, sir. How many in your party?” Brady asked.

“Just me and for one night only. I would also like a bath and shave. And is there a laundry in town? My clothes are getting a mite ripe from bein’ on the trail. Nathan over at the livery said ta mention his name.”

Brady Hooks wrinkled his nose in agreement with the clothes being ripe said, “Nathan is a good man. Your horse will be well taken care of, no worry about that. The laundry and bath are one in the same. They’re run by a Chinaman, Charlie Woo, three doors down to your left as you go out the door. Do you want the ground floor or do you prefer to be upstairs? The price is the same.” Brady seemed anxious to get back to his nap. Must have been an interesting dream, Clay thought to himself.

“Ground floor is just fine. How much?”

“One dollar.”

As Clay laid a silver dollar on the counter, Brady Hooks handed him a key and said, “Room 105.”

Both Clay and the hotel clerk turned at the sound of lightning striking somewhere nearby.

"Good night to be in out of the rain. It's that time of year. But it seems we've had more than is normal this year," Brady said, shaking his head.

Clay nodded his head and headed down the hallway.

The room was clean sparse. A double bed with a feather tic mattress stood against one wall. On the opposite wall was a stand with two drawers. On top was a bowl for washing and next to it, a pitcher filled with water. A bar of soap sat in a dish next to the bowl and a towel hung on a hook above and to the side of the stand. Above the stand was a mirror for shaving and combing your hair. There was a rocking chair near the window and several hooks on the wall to hang up your clothes, if you had extra, and that was it.

Not Wichita or Dallas it would do. Clay tossed his saddlebags on the bed and gave a long sigh, wondering to himself if he should take this time for himself? But the truth was, he was tired and if he didn't get at least a little rest, he would do the ladies no good, and probably get himself killed to boot. He left the room, locking the door behind him.

Clay stepped out of the hotel and stopped. A cold wind slapped him in the face and for just a moment, he wondered again if he was on a fool's errand. The thought was there and then it was gone. There would be no turning back; not until he had rescued the women and hopefully punished the men who had taken them from their homes.

As he entered the Chinese laundry, large drops of rain began to fall. A small bell attached to the door announced his arrival.

At the sound of the bell, Charlie Woo, a man who you knew by looking at him, had not missed many meals, came bounding through a curtain that hid the back room and laundry. Grinning broadly, he took two steps toward Clay and stopped. The smile disappeared and he wrinkled his nose. “No need explain, Charlie know why you come to my laundry and bath; fifty cents for bath - plenty hot water, you bet. Ten cents for shave, and seventy-five cents for laundry – wash and iron. That come to one dollar, fifty cents, prease.”

Clay didn’t argue with Charlie and his poor adding abilities, it would be worth a dollar and a half to get a bath and into clean clothes, again. Besides, he figured Charlie Woo was very good at math and knew exactly what he was doing. Most of the cowboys who came into his laundry could barely read or sign their names, so he would test them and more than likely, made a little extra money from time to time.

An hour later, as he stood drying himself off, he figured the bath alone was worth a buck and a half. Charlie Woo knew how to give his customers their money’s worth.

The beautiful, young Asian girl who had shaved him, had also brought him a cigar and a tall glass of beer – all part of the dollar fifty and for an extra two dollars she had climbed into the large tub with him.

It had been a long time since he’d been with a woman, let alone one as young and beautiful as this young lady was, so he didn’t object, nor was he disappointed.

While he was drying himself, a second young lady came in with his clean and pressed clothes and hung them on a wall hook. With the towel wrapped around him, Clay stepped over to the bench where his personal belongings lay and retrieved a small bag containing his silver money. He took a one-dollar silver piece and handed it to the young lady who bowed several times as she backed out of the room, smiling.

That may have been the largest tip she'd received today. Cowboys normally didn't have a lot of money, so they weren't big on tipping.

Clay took his time and got dressed. He was quickly beginning to like Antelope Wells. He felt clean and whole again. Although he hadn't picked up any information to speak of so far, he was sure if there was any to be had, he would get it at the cantina.

The cantina was across the street from Charlie Woo's. Clay could hear Mexican music coming out of the open doorway as he hurried across the street that was quickly turning to mud.

The cantina was typical of a border town; a long bar where men stood to drink and talk. Across from the bar, were several tables where gambling took place or women of the evening sat with the lonely men and encouraged them to drink, then suggested they accompany them to one of the back rooms where, for a price, she would show him how wonderful life could be.

Fortunately, Clay would not need their services, he'd been well taken care of over at Charlie Woo's and he didn't feel guilty. There was yet to be anything other than one kiss between him and the Senora, and nothing had actually been said.

No one paid much attention as he sauntered over to the end of the bar and rested his elbows on it and waited for Lopez to see him. He looked like just another cowboy in off the trail, looking for a drink.

Apparently, Lopez had a wide peripheral vision because he immediately turned from what he was doing and hurried down to the end of the bar.

"Senor', you are new in town. I am Lopez, owner of this fine establishment. What can I get you? The first one is on the house."

"Just a beer, and thanks," Clay said as Lopez left to get his beer. He had come to the right place. If anyone knew whether or not a prison wagon loaded with women had come through town, it would be Lopez.

When Lopez returned with the glass of beer, he said, "Welcome to Antelope Wells, will you be staying long?"

Clay took a long sip of the beer. It tasted good and he let it settle in his stomach before he answered. "No, just passin' through. I'm kinda lookin' for someone and you could maybe help. You seem to be a man who sees and hears things."

Lopez's chest swelled up with pride. "Maybe I could help you, depending on what you want to know and why. If something goes on in this town, I usually know about it. In my cantina there is much talk."

"Figured as much," Clay said as he drank down his beer and set the glass on the bar. "Another one and this time I pay."

Lopez understood the meaning behind the stranger's words and as he turned to go fill up the glass again, he called over his shoulder, "Si, Senor'."

This time, when he set the glass of beer in front of Clay, there was ten dollars in silver lying on the bar. Lopez looked Clay in the eyes and asked, "What is it you wish to know, Senor'?"

"Been following the tracks of a large wagon, possibly one of them prison wagons, and maybe loaded with women prisoners. Just wondering if such ah wagon might have come through town?"

"I see," Lopez said, eyeing him carefully. "And may I ask, why you are following this wagon you call, a prison wagon?"

"If you're wonderin' if I'm the law, I'm not. I'm an angry husband. Ya see, some slavers kidnapped my wife and I want her back. I been tryin' to catch up with them for some time now, and this morning, those tracks led me here. I'd be much obliged if you could tell me anything."

After what seemed to be a long pause, Lopez smiled and said, "Senor', I like you and I believe what you have said, so I will tell you what I know."

Lopez held up his hand indicating he needed a moment to wait on some of his other customers and while he was gone, Clay quietly sipped on his beer as he added another ten dollars to the money on the bar.

When Lopez returned, he glanced at the pile of money and noticed it had grown. Next, he took a hard look at the man standing across the bar from him. This would not be a man to have as an enemy, he decided. In that instant, Lopez decided he liked this gringo, and decided to be honest with him. "I like the way you do business, Senor'. Yes, there was a wagon like you described. It came through town a few days ago. And Si, it was full of women, prisoners who were on their way to Matamoras to be deported."

"Why Matamoras?" Clay asked. And not Mexico City, he wondered.

"Because ships captains and other men come to the slave auctions there. Some of the women will go to nearby plantations, some will become concubines, while others will go to South America and be sold there for a huge profit, or so I'm told" Lopez said with a shrug of his shoulders.

"And did he offer to sell any of them to you?" Clay asked as he looked at Lopez over the rim of his glass.

Lopez looked at Clay and said, "Senor', you are a very wise man. Si, he did say some of them were whores I might use in my establishment. And Si, he told me I could purchase them for one hundred dollars apiece, in silver or gold."

"And how many did you buy?" Clay asked as he set the glass on the bar.

Lopez looked at Clay, and shaking his head, he said, "Senor', as I have said, you are a very wise man. There are three of them upstairs, all very beautiful women I must tell you, this man who did not give his name, lied to me because not even one of them is a whore. In fact, they all refused to do my bidding even after I threatened to beat them if they did not do as I said."

"And did you beat them?" Clay asked.

Lopez looked into the man's eyes and felt a stab of fear run through him. "No, Senor', I am not a woman beater. I was hoping a threat would work it didn't."

Clay studied Lopez for a moment, and then asked, "May I see them – talk to them?" His heart was racing he tried not to show his feelings. He was glad Lopez had not harmed the women because if he had… He let the thought drop because there was no reason to go there – at least not right now. He would wait until he saw the women.

Lopez nodded his head. "Si Senor'. Only… I hope you will not hold it against me if one of them is the woman you seek."

Clay finished his beer and set the glass on the bar. "No, I don't reckon I can hold you responsible for somethin' you knew nothin' about," he said, shoveling the small pile of silver coins across the bar toward Lopez. "Here, take this. You've earned it."

Lopez shoved the pile of coins back in Clay's direction. "Not yet, Senor'. Let us wait until you have talked to the women upstairs. If you are satisfied, then I will accept your money."

As they walked up the stairs, Clay said, "Actually, I'm hopin' one of them is my wife."

Lopez nodded his head; beads of sweat were popping out on his forehead. "Si, I hope so too."

At the door, Lopez stopped, took a deep breath, made the sign of the cross and then opened the door.

Standing on the far side of the room stood three women, the one in front was holding a piece of broken chair leg with both hands, ready to defend herself and the two women standing behind her.

"You come close to us and it is you who will get a beating," Victoria said as she raised the club even higher.

Clay was grinning from ear to ear as he stepped around Lopez and stared at the three women. "Ain't nobody gonna beat on you or do anything else to you," he said with an easy drawl.

For a moment, Victoria couldn't believe her eyes. Was it really him? Her heart began to beat fast and a chill ran through her, and before she realized what she was doing, she dropped the club, raced across the room and flung her arms around his neck and was kissing him all over his face. "Oh Clay, you don't know how happy I am to see you. I hoped and prayed after this much time… I… I thought you were dead!"

Clay wrapped his arms around her and realized how good she felt, and when he could finally get a word in, he said, "Reckon I'm not as easy ta kill as folks might think."

They looked into each other's eyes and began to laugh.

Lopez breathed a sigh of relief and stepped close to Clay and Victoria.

When Clay noticed him, Lopez said, "I am so glad one of these fine ladies is your wife, Senor'."

Clay and Victoria looked at each other and began to laugh all over again, as Lopez stood next to them with a confused look on his face.

Clay told the women to get ready to leave, then took Lopez out into the hallway where he gave him the twenty dollars in silver he'd promised.

"Gracias, Senor'. I am glad I could help."

"Yes. But now, we have another matter to discuss."

"And what would that be?" Lopez asked, knowing full well what Clay was talking about. He wanted to buy the women back.

Clay scratched the back of his neck. "I think you already know what I'm going to say. It's just a matter of how much? I have no problem with you making a small profit, just don't try to take advantage of me just because one of the women is my wife."

"Senor'! I am wounded that you think I would try to take advantage of a situation so delicate as this one. Two hundred dollars each; gold or silver."

Clay grinned, knowing Lopez opened the negotiations higher than he expected to get. "One hundred ten dollars each."

Senor', for you, one hundred seventy-five dollars each."

Clay decided he'd haggled long enough. "One hundred fifty dollars in silver and that's my final offer."

"You are indeed a good trader, mi amigo," Lopez said and stuck out his hand.

After the handshake to seal the deal, Clay counted out four hundred fifty dollars from his bag of silver coins.

Lopez eyed the bag and then looked back at Clay and dec leave well enough alone. This would not be a man to have as your enem He would not try to steal the rest of the gringo's money. Besides, he already was having a good day – the bar was full of drinking cowboys, his three ladies were plying their trade, he'd gotten twenty dollars for his information, he'd gotten his money back for the women, plus making a hundred and fifty-dollar profit. Not a bad day. Not a bad day at all, he thought to himself.

CHAPTER TWENTY-SIX

Back at the hotel, Clay rented two more rooms, one for the Senora and one for the other two ladies. One was white and in her early twenties, who said her name was Barbara Conway. She'd been abducted from a stagecoach just northwest of Roswell. She was on her way to see her sick aunt. The other one was a Mexican girl in her late teens. She didn't speak English but said her name was Conchita Flores. She said her father raised a small herd of sheep, not far from the town of Carrizozo – just her and her younger brother and their mother and father. Her father and brother had been off tending the sheep when the men arrived on horseback. They were drunk and ransacked the small house and found her father's tequila and drank it, then grabbed her and her mother and raped them. When the one who had raped her mother was finished with her, he pulled his pistol and shot her. Next, they tied her to the only horse her father owned and took her away. It had been several days before they met up with the others and each night, they took turns abusing her. Once they met up with the others, they threw her into the wagon with the other women.

By the time she had finished, she was trembling and crying like a child. Victoria and the woman named Barbara Conway, put their arms around her and told her over and over that everything would be fine, now.

Both women were so relieved to be free again, they couldn't stop crying and repeatedly thanked Clay over and over, until he held up his hands and said, "Thank you ladies you've thanked me enough." It was to the point where it was embarrassing. "Now, please, make yourselves presentable and we'll all go out and get some supper."

Clay wanted to get Victoria alone and explain about the wife thing didn't get a chance until Victoria had promised the women that they were safe now and she would make sure they got back to their homes, safe and sound.

Suddenly, the women's admirations switched from Clay to Victoria. While he was glad about that, he still needed to talk to Victoria, alone.

"Ladies, I need to talk to the Senora and you need some time before we go to supper." And with that, he took Victoria by the arm and escorted her into the hallway before the other women could protest.

In the hallway, Clay wasted no time. "Ah, about that wife business..."

Victoria stopped and faced him. There was a smile on her face and a gleam in her eyes. "No need to explain. You said and did what you had to do to. I'm just glad there was no killing involved. And I'm very glad you were not killed and came looking for us. I still can't believe you found us!"

"There were a few times when storms washed out the tracks I got lucky and found them, again."

"It was not luck. It was how you are. You do not start something you do not finish. So, when will you be going after the rest of the women?" Victoria asked with a look of concern on her face.

For a moment, Clay was confused. Up to this point, his only concern was to get Victoria back. "Are you suggesting what I think you're suggesting?" Clay asked with a look of shock on his face.

Victoria took him by the arm as they walked to the door of her room. At the door she released his arm and looked him in the eyes. "Si, yes. That is exactly what I'm hoping you will do. There are some women out there who are scared and have nothing to look forward to except slavery or prostitution, which amounts to the same thing. They need you Clay."

Clay scrunched up his nose and scratched his neck. "Why don't we discuss this after we've had some supper? It's been a long day and I'm hungry."

"Alright," Victoria said, "but I don't know of anyone else who could find them and rescue them from those horrible men."

"I'll meet you ladies in the lobby in ten minutes," Clay said as he turned and walked toward his room, needing some time to think.

When they walked into the restaurant, the place was close to being full. Clay saw a table for four back in the far corner and escorted the ladies in that direction. As they passed a table filled with rough looking cowboys, one of them grabbed Barbara by the arm and jerked her down on his lap and looked up at Clay.

"Looks like you can spare this one. Word is you bought'em from Lopez. Got yer own thing goin'. I'll give you ten dollars for her, for the night, of course."

Clay stopped and looked down at the man, and then over at Barbara, whose eyes were wild with fear. He hadn't planned for something like this realized that in a border town, he should have.

Clay looked at Victoria and said, "You take the ladies back to the table and I'll be along shortly."

He then reached over and helped Barbara off the man's lap, saying, "Sure, big fella. But first, she needs a meal and we need to discuss the deal, outside. I don't like doin' business in front of people."

The huge cowboy jumped up with his fists closed tightly and was about to object Clay raised both hands up, palms forward.

"Not lookin for trouble, cowboy; specially with a man as big as you. But you have ta understand, these women are special and there are rules."

"Rules?" the big cowboy said.

Clay pushed Barbara toward Victoria and the young Mexican girl, whispering, "Don't worry, everything will be alright."

"What'ya say ta her?" the big cowboy demanded.

"I just told her ta go have some supper while you and I go outside and discuss the details," Clay said as he headed for the door, hoping the man would follow him.

Sure enough, as Clay stepped onto the sidewalk, the big cowboy was right behind him.

"I still ain't clear about them rules you keep talkin' about. I offered ah fair price, so what's there ta dicker about?"

A few steps down the sidewalk, out of view from the restaurant, Clay stopped and turned around. Looking up at the big cowboy, he thought, "this is the biggest man I've ever had ta deal with." There was no doubt the man was a brawler, and that he'd probably never lost a fight, would be a fair assumption.

"Rules," Clay said. "Yes sir, rules."

The big cowboy shook his head. "There ain't no rules in beddin' ah prostitute."

"It's like this," Clay said, trying to decide how to go about not getting his neck broken while explaining that he wouldn't be spending the night with her. "It's like this, I'm the owner; you know, the one who decides who she sleeps with and for how much."

The big cowboy nodded his head in agreement. "Yes sir, I understand."

"Good, yes, that's very good, because it's like this - the woman is not for sale or rent to you or anyone else."

It took a moment for the information to sink in and when it did, the big cowboy reared back and gave off with a loud roar of laughter. But when the laugh ended, he looked down at Clay and Clay could see the fire in the man's eyes.

"Well then," the big cowboy said, "I reckon I'm just gonna half'ta whup up on you until you beg me ta take the woman off yer hands fer nuthin'."

Clay tried hard to get a confused look on his face. "You mean you want to fight?" Clay asked.

"I don't reckon they'll be much fightin' to it," the big cowboy said. "The way I see it, there'll only be two hits. I hit you and you hit the ground." And with this he roared with laughter, again.

"Ok, ok," Clay said with a big grin. "But before we do, you remember those rules I spoke of before?"

The big cowboy nodded his head yes, and said, "Uh huh."

"And what is your name? I hate talkin to somebody without knowin his name."

"Rufus. My name is Rufus Crow, like them birds."

Clay raised both hands in the air, palms forward. "Good. Now Rufus Crow, like the birds, the first rule is, no kicking in the groin, like this," he said as he kicked the big cowboy between the legs.

Rufus Crow let out a loud groan and bent over, grabbing his crotch.

"Now, rule number two is, none of this," he said as he reached over and grabbed Rufus by both ears and slammed his face down against his up thrust knee. Clay heard the man's nose break and stepped back before the blood began to flow.

Next, Clay stepped to the side and grabbed Rufus by his shirt collar and by his belt and drove him forward as hard as he could, driving his head against the wooden side of the building. "And definitely none of this."

Rufus staggered back two steps, then plopped down on his rear and like a slow falling tree, fell backwards onto his back, blood running from his nose and staining the big man's shirt.

Clay stood there only a moment before he nudged Rufus with the toe of his boot and said, "Rufus, you awake?" When Rufus didn't reply, Clay started back for the restaurant, talking to himself. "Sometimes when facin' insurmountable odds, you just have to lay down the rules."

Inside the restaurant, Clay glanced down at the other cowboys at Rufus' table and said, "He changed his mind. He decided he didn't want the woman."

As Clay continued on toward where the three ladies were sitting, the cowboys jumped up and headed for the door.

Clay hadn't had time to do anything except order his supper when the three cowboys came back into the restaurant and marched straight over to him.

The one in the lead, a tall, well-built man of about thirty who wore his gun low like a gunfighter does, walked up to Clay and stopped. Clay noticed the man had removed the leather thong that held his pistol in its holster. This was not a good sign. The man was looking for trouble and that was the last thing Clay wanted right now, especially in a restaurant filled with people. Some innocent bystander could get hurt or possibly even killed if things got hot and heavy.

Clay stood up with his left side facing the man so the man would not see him lift the thong from his own pistol. Clay wasn't looking for gunplay he wanted to be ready just in case.

Clay looked the man in the eyes and asked, "Somethin' I can do for you?"

"Yeah," the man said. "You can start by telling me how you whipped Rufus. How many men did you have out there, waitin' to jump him?"

"I don't know you from Adam and I don't see that what went on between me and Rufus is any of your concern since you asked, I'll tell you this much. It was just me and Rufus and no one else. Didn't need any help with the likes of him."

The gunfighter made a smirking noise and said, "I don't believe you. Ain't no man your size ever whipped Rufus. In fact, I ain't never seen Rufus whipped by anybody."

"He is a right good sized fella; I'll give him that. But to be honest, he isn't much in the brain department, so whippin' him wasn't too difficult."

"I think you're a liar!" the gunslinger yelled. "And I'm here ta back up my words with my gun."

Clay sighed. "I was hopin' it wouldn't come ta that. Maybe we should go outside, seein' that there is a lot of innocent bystanders in here who might accidentally get themselves hurt."

The gunslinger, thinking Clay was stalling, turned to his friends and said with a smirk, "I told ya he'd back down or try ta lure me outside where his friends would be ah waitin'."

He turned back to Clay and said, "No. It's gonna happen right here so these good folks can see you for the low down coward you are."

Clay's eyes went cold and his voice had no nonsense to it. "Mister, you go for that hog-leg and it will be the last time you do."

The gunfighter wasn't ready for this kind of response and he took another hard look at Clay. The man was anything but scared or nervous and suddenly he wasn't so sure of himself. Could this man be as good with a gun as he was with his fists, or was he just full of bravado? He sure didn't look like a gunfighter.

Taking a deep breath, he knew he couldn't back out now, and went for his gun. Before he cleared leather, he was staring down the barrel of

Clay's pistol. The man was pure lightning fast and he knew he'd picked on the wrong man.

Slowly, the gunfighter dropped his pistol back into his holster and raised his hands. "Guess I made a mistake, mister. My apologies," his eyes blazing daggers. He hated being humiliated in front of his two friends and the people in the restaurant.

"We all make mistakes from time to time. Be glad I'm in a generous mood. If there is ever ah next time, and I hope there won't be, I won't hesitate. You understand what I'm sayin'?"

The gunslinger nodded his head. "I understand you can bet there will be a next time, and I'll be ready for you," he said with a bit of bravado to show his friends and the people in the restaurant he still considered himself to be the top gun in these parts.

Clay stared at the man, understanding his humiliation and was trying desperately to think of something to say to diffuse the situation when the Senora spoke up.

"Senor', do you know who this man is?"

Clay turned and gave her a stern look.

Slick Haines, as the gunfighter was known as, grinned and said, "No ma'am, don't reckon I do. Is he supposed ta be somebody special?"

"Some people might say that."

Clay was still trying to give her a stern look of disapproval she ignored him.

"Did you hear about the man who took on the Curly Beeler gang single-handed, and won?"

Slick glanced at his friends and then back to the Senora. "I think it's safe ta say that we all heard the story it's hard ta believe that one man could waltz inta town and best Curly and all his men. Those was some mighty tough hombres that rode with him. Besides, what's that got ta do with anything?"

The Senora smiled and said, "Well it's true. I know because I happened to be in town on business that day and witnessed the whole thing. And the reason I bring it up is because the man who killed Curly and his men without getting so much as a scratch is standing right in front of you."

She let this information sink in for a moment, then continued. "Now, if you still feel so inclined, think twice before you do something stupid. I do not think you are ready to die, Senor'."

Slick felt a knot in the pit of his stomach. The fact was, everybody in the town had sworn Curly and his men were killed by one man, who then got on his horse and rode away, with not a word ta anybody.

"Is what the lady said, true? Did you ride inta town and shoot down Curly and his men, then ride away like nuthin' had happened?"

"I had my reasons for doin' what I did. I can't say I'm proud of myself for what I did like I said, I had my reasons. And I don't have any reason ta kill you, unless you force me to."

Slick Haines stood there, staring at the man who had earlier, out drawn him hadn't pulled the trigger and he felt relieved to have survived the situation. "You won't have any more trouble out of me," he said as he turned and walked toward the front of the restaurant.

Clay watched until they reached the front door before he decided to sit down. But as he was sitting down and in an awkward position, Slick Haines whirled and at the same time, drew his pistol.

When the smoke cleared, Clay was standing next to the table with his gun in his hand, staring at Slick Haines who was sitting on the floor, slumped against the door with a red spot of blood on his shirt over where his heart was located.

Clay looked around the restaurant at the stunned faces staring back and forth between him and Slick Haines, who would no longer be a threat to them.

Clay dropped his pistol back into his holster and said, “I’m really sorry you had ta witness this. I didn’t want it ta happen and I hope it won’t spoil your meal.”

Clay looked toward the door and said to the other two cowboys, “Get him out of here and tell your oversized friend to let things be. I don’t want any more trouble , if it comes huntin’ me, I won’t back down.”

In the space of five minutes, the two cowboys had carried their friend outside and the restaurant had settled back down.

When the lady brought their food, Clay whispered to her that he would be picking up everyone’s meal ticket. She smiled and said, “Thank you that isn’t necessary, you did this town a big favor. Those men have lorded over us for some time now and not once did they ever pay for a meal.”

Clay nodded and said, “It’s good ta know that I could be of some help I still plan on picking up the bill.”

Back in Clay’s room at the hotel, he laid out his plan to put the ladies on the stage with tickets back to where they came from along with money for food. Turning to Victoria he said, “If it’s alright with you, I will sell the mule and ride along on horseback, or trail the two horses behind the stagecoach. That way I’ll be around in case there’s any more trouble.”

He was hoping she'd forgotten about the idea of sending him after the other women that was like thinking she'd ever forget being abducted.

"What about the other women?" Victoria protested.

"What if it was your daughter or wife? Wouldn't you want someone to go after them, if you couldn't?" Barbara interjected.

Clay felt a pang of guilt and shook his head. They were right he couldn't believe he was allowing these three women to railroad him into committing suicide.

"What if we telegraph the authorities down in Matamoras and inform them of what's going on?" Barbara asked. "Wouldn't they do something? Hold the women until you could get there?"

It took Clay the better part of an hour to explain that telegraphing the authorities in Matamoras would be a waste of time. "Not only wouldn't they do anything about it, they're more than likely paid to look the other way."

Conchita and Barbara were flabbergasted and hard pressed to believe that officers of the law could be bought off from doing their duty.

"Are sheriffs and town marshals not to be trusted, then?" Barbara asked. "And what about, judges?"

It took Clay another hour to explain how not all lawmen were crooked, and that in many places, paying a lawman to look the other way, was a regular thing – especially down in Mexico.

Victoria, being more of a woman of the world, had heard and seen this happen and told the others that what Clay said was true.

"Well if that's true, then it's all the more reason Mister Brentwood should go down there and get those women and bring them back. If he doesn't, who will?" Barbara said.

At that point, the Senora stated that she would pay him to go down and try to bring the women back, if he could.

Clay gave a sigh and shook his head. He knew he couldn't accept the Senora's money and he said so.

"Senora, I don't want your money. If I decide to go after them, it will be because it's the right thing to do."

The women folded their arms across their chests and stared at him. He was whipped and he knew it.

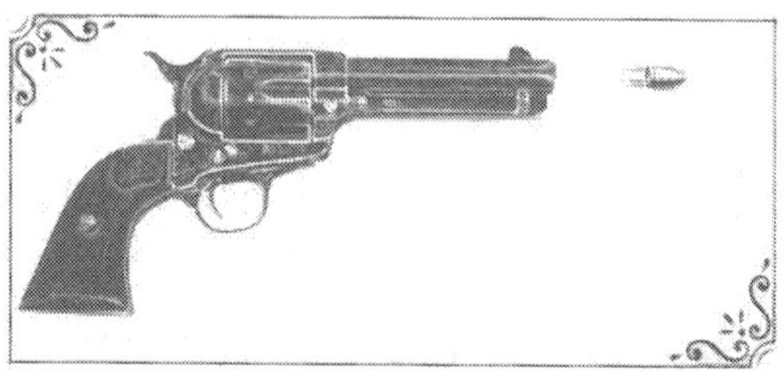

CHAPTER TWENTY-SEVEN

-

The following morning, after breakfast, all the women went to Charlie Woo's for a bath and have their clothes cleaned for the long trip, and since none of the women had any money, Clay paid Charlie, who made big eyes at Clay when he brought in three women. Clay left, shaking his head. He made arrangements for them to get back home. The stage would leave somewhere between four and five this afternoon.

When the other two women had said their goodbyes and had gone back to the hotel to wait, Victoria took Clay by the arm and walked him to a shady area between two of the buildings.

She took his hands and said, "I don't know the words that describe how I feel at this moment. I haven't known many men the few I have known, other than my father, cannot come close to being the man you are, Senor' Clay Brentwood."

Clay interrupted her and said "Hold on. This isn't necessary right now. You're feelin' grateful about now and you might say somethin' you'll regret later on. Why don't you just let things rest until you get back home, and can think things through, and when I get back we can sit down and talk this all out. What'ya say?"

She looked at him with loving eyes and nodded her head in agreement.

He walked her to the door of the hotel and said his goodbyes there, handing her a bag with silver coins in it. "In case you need it," he said as he leaned over and lightly kissed her on the forehead.

Before she could react, he was off the sidewalk and heading for the livery stable where his horses and mule were waiting, packed and ready to go.

A few minutes later, Clay left Antelope Wells, heading south for Matamoras. Only this time he wasn't as concerned about hunting for wagon tracks. This time he knew where he was headed – a one-thousand-mile trek to Matamoras. He hoped he would catch up with them long before.

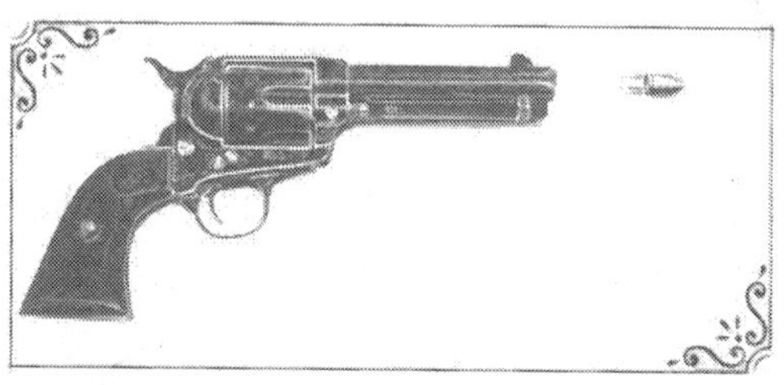

CHAPTER TWENTY-EIGHT

-

Riding along at a steady pace so as not to wear the animals down, Clay rolled and smoked a cigarette, wondering how he'd let himself get badgered into making this insane trip.

But the truth was, he would have felt guilty if he hadn't. And he had to agree, if not him, who would be risking their life to go after someone who was already lost to them; probably no one, which was sad. By now, the women were feeling like their world had ended – and maybe some of them were even contemplating taking their own lives rather than living the rest of their days as slaves or prostitutes.

Rounding a curve in the road that led past a small mesa, Clay saw two people in the distance. From their peon clothing and sombreros, it looked like a Mexican man and a boy. Suddenly, the hair on the back of Clay's neck stood on end and he put his heels into the black stallion's ribs, urging him into a gallop.

When the man and the boy heard the horses coming, they stopped and turned around. Both were armed; the man held a rifle and the boy had a machete. The sun had not yet reached its zenith, so they had to squint to see.

When Clay came abreast of them, he pulled his animals to a halt. As Clay stared down at them, there was no doubt in his mind; this was Conchita's father and brother. The boy was carrying a water bag and the man had a sack slung over his shoulder with what Clay believed to be what little food they had.

"Habla English?" Clay asked.

Both the man and the boy shook their heads, 'no.'

"No problemo," Clay said in Mexican. And again, in their native tongue, he asked if their names were, Flores, which of course he was sure it was.

Both, the man and the boy, got surprised looks on their faces as they pulled off their sombreros. "Si Senor, I am Hector Flores and this is my son, Juan. We have come a long way. We are on a journey to find my daughter who was stolen from us. We have been following the wagon tracks of the men who raped and killed my wife and took my only daughter. I think by now she is very afraid."

Clay smiled, knowing he had guessed right.

Hector Flores continued. "I am surprised you speak our language and even more surprised you know my name. How is that, Senor'?"

Clay stepped from the saddle and walked over and stood in front of Conchita's father. "I know who you are because I have talked with Conchita and she has told me about you. Like you, I too search for the men who steal women to sell them as slaves in the fields, or, as prostitutes. But as far as your daughter is concerned, you do not have to worry. She is safe and well, a few miles back in the town of Antelope Wells. If we are to get back there before she leaves on the stage to go home, we must hurry. Quickly, both of you climb aboard the other horse and let us go as quickly as we can."

Without hesitation, both the man and the boy climbed aboard the steel-dust and they headed back for Antelope Wells as fast as Clay dared to push his animals.

Clay figured if they could get back in time, Conchita would be happily re-united with her father and brother, and especially glad to know they had come hunting for her. Then a thought occurred to him. Are there others out there hunting down the men who stole their women? Will I meet up with them, also, he wondered?

The stage had just pulled up in front of the hotel as Clay, Senor' Flores and Juan rode down the street at a fast pace. The three women were coming out of the hotel and stopped at the sound of Clay's voice. "Victoria, don't let Conchita board the stage, yet."

At the sound of her name, Conchita looked toward them, and for a moment her face was frozen with a look of confusion when she saw her father and brother, a smile spread across her face. She lifted her skirt and raced down the street toward them, stopping only when the steel-dust slid to a halt in front of her.

Her father and brother jumped off the horse and hardly a moment later, the three of them were hugging, laughing and crying all at the same time.

Victoria stepped off the sidewalk and hurried over to where Clay sat on the black stallion. She looked up at him, smiling and shaking her head. "You are an amazing man, Senor' Clay Brentwood. How did you go about this miracle?"

Clay felt his face redden as he reached into his depleting sack of silver coins and pulled out several of them and handed them to the Senora. "I reckon this will be enough to get her father and the boy home, too," he said, evading her question.

"You're not going to answer my question, are you?" she asked.

"I've already lost a lot of daylight. I'd best be movin' on," Clay said. And with that, he whirled the horses around and was heading back down the street when he heard Conchita call his name. "Senor' Clay!"

Clay gently nudged the black stallion with his heels, urging him into a trot and without stopping or looking back; he lifted his hat and waved it in the air. He'd had enough, "I can't thank you enough," tearful sentiments to last him a lifetime. Besides, he was burning daylight.

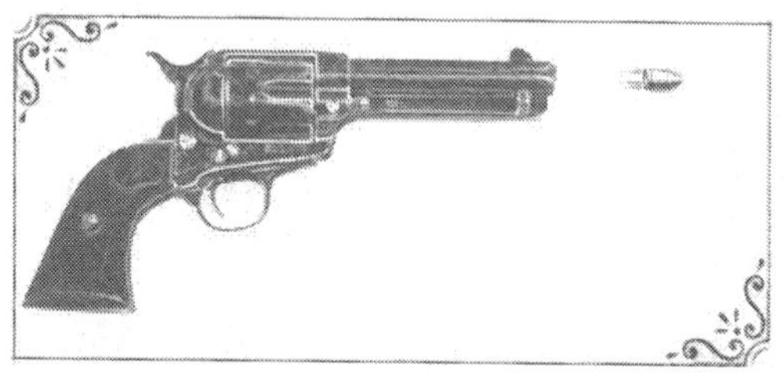

CHAPTER TWENTY-NINE

-

Three nights later, Clay Brentwood camped out in the open under a sky filled with stars for as far as the eyes could see. Clay sat next to his fire, sipping on a cup of coffee and feeling very small. The moon was full and round and looked so close that it made you feel you could ride right onto it if you rode over the horizon. He could see the moon's mountains and craters. And as he watched, a shooting star streaked across the sky.

Before he climbed into his bedroll, Clay wondered about this world he lived on and all the things he would never understand. How far away were the stars? Was there life on any of them, and would man ever travel out there to find out?

Two minutes after pulling the wool blanket up to his chin to stave off the chill of the night, the rumbling of his snoring, carried by the wind, caused a coyote, some distance away, to raise its head and sniff the air. Not feeling threatened by Clay's snoring; the coyote lifted his head even higher and howled at the moon that shone down on both of them.

Breakfast consisted of hot coffee, bacon, beans and a fried potato – the last one he had. He didn't take time to make biscuits or gravy, he was anxious to get on the trail.

Clay was about to break camp when once again the hair on the back of his neck stood on end. He hesitated just a moment, letting his ears listen for any unusual sound. He heard nothing - but after a moment, his nose picked up a human smell. An old Indian who had worked for him on his ranch back in Texas had taught him how to do this.

"Everything has its own smell," the old man had said. And if your nose is trained properly, you can detect such smells. And now, Clay was detecting the smell of fear. He couldn't explain how he could do this, he just could.

Slowly, so as not to spook whoever was near, Clay turned his head and smiled as he looked into the eyes of a young Indian boy, not more than ten years old. The boy was standing stock still, no more than fifty or sixty feet from Clay's camp. How he'd gotten this close without Clay hearing him, only attributed to the fact that he was an Indian.

Clay raised both hands in the air, palms forward to show he meant no harm, then motioned for the boy to come forward, pointing in the direction of the skillet, which still had food in it. Clay hadn't been as hungry as he'd thought he was.

When the boy just stood there, Clay turned back, and without saying anything, went over to the horses and began saddling the black. Glancing over his shoulder, Clay grinned. The boy was squatted next to the skillet and was cramming food into his mouth as fast as he could.

After saddling his horse and putting the packsaddle on the mule, Clay looked back toward the boy, who was now standing and staring at him. "Buenos Dais," Clay said in Spanish. Since most of the Indians he knew of spoke Spanish, along with their own language, and not knowing what tribe the boy was from, he tried Spanish first.

The boy just stared at him.

"Do you speak English?" Clay then asked.

After a long moment while the boy was deciding whether to trust this gringo, or not, the boy nodded his head, yes.

The boy is scared, not trusting of anyone. He understood this why, Clay wondered. Clay looked around saw no others.

"Good," Clay said in English. "You have nothing to fear from me. I will not harm you. I am riding south, and if you want to, you can ride along with me."

When the boy said nothing, Clay walked over and finished breaking camp and loaded the mule. When he was ready to leave, he pointed in the direction of the steel-dust.

After only a moment's hesitation, the Indian boy walked over and mounted the steel-dust and took up its reins.

Clay was sitting astride the black stallion holding his breath, wondering if the boy would take off, trying to steal the horse. That he could catch him wasn't the issue. The black stallion could out run any horse he'd ever come up against, even the steel-dust, who could run almost as fast as the black. The boy sat there, waiting on Clay to move out.

When the boy didn't race away, Clay hauled up on the mule's lead rope and nudged the black down the road.

After less than a quarter of a mile, the boy rode up next to Clay and kept pace. Clay glanced his way and smiled, then turned his head back toward the direction they were going, allowing the boy time and space, hoping he would come to trust him and maybe talk.

Like almost every other day, it was hot and dusty. During this whole trip, Clay had seen very few people and not one of them on horseback. They were either Mexican peasants who were walking in the opposite direction, barefoot and in rags, or twice, he had met up with older Mexican men who were riding donkeys. And not one of them looked him in the eyes as they passed. And now, here he was, straddled with a boy who didn't talk.

The sun was close to noontime when Clay stopped under the lea of an overhang sticking out from a small mound of sand and rock. He stepped down and loosened the saddles on the black and the mule, then gave each one a drink of water from a canvas bucket he carried on the pack for this purpose.

Since the boy was riding bareback, he had no saddle to loosen when Clay was finished watering the black and the mule, the boy held out his hand for the bucket and when Clay gave it to him, he poured a small portion of water into it and watered the steel-dust.

Clay squatted in the shade and pulled out a small sack of beef jerky and removed two pieces. He began chewing on one of them, and when the boy came close, he stuck out the other piece in the boy's direction.

Without a word, the boy took the piece of jerky, and then squatted down next to Clay and bit off a piece and began to chew, enjoying the salty taste of the dried meat.

When they finished the jerky, Clay handed his canteen to the boy, who took a long pull and then handed it back.

Clay then stood up and tightened the cinches on the black and the mule. The boy was already mounted and ready to go when Clay stepped into the saddle.

For three days, this is how it went. The boy would do his share, like gathering firewood when they stopped for the night, or helping clean up the camp and looked after the steel-dust uttered not a word.

The morning of the fourth day they broke camp as usual and headed down the dusty road. After about a mile, without any warning, the boy said, "Some very bad men stole my sisters, She Who Sings and Pretty Bird. I am going to find the bad men and get my sisters back."

Clay had just rolled a smoke and had taken a puff, when the boy decided to talk. Clay took his time, blowing out the smoke slowly while he thought about what the boy said. So, once again he had run into someone else who was hunting the slavers a boy no more than ten? That he had not expected. At least now he understood the boy's reluctance to trust anyone.

Without looking at the boy, Clay said, "Sounds like we're chasing after the same bad men. I'm looking for them too. But I'm wonderin', why you are out here alone? Where are your people? Your father? Do you have any brothers? You're kinda young to be out here searchin' for bad men all by yourself."

Tears were forming in his eyes and he tried to fight them back. "My mother and my father were killed by the bad men when they tried to stop them from taking my sisters. I have no brothers. They would have taken me too, if I had not run away and hid."

"I see," Clay said as he blew another stream of smoke into the air. "You are very brave how do you expect to save your sisters? You will be going against some very bad men, and you don't even have a gun that I can see."

"I do not know," the boy admitted. "But I am the man of my family now and it is my job to find them and bring them home."

"If I might ask, how many winters have you seen and where did you learn to speak English so well?"

Puffing out his chest, the boy said, "I am ten and I learned to read, write and speak English from the missionaries. I also speak Spanish and my native tongue, which is Luiseno. It was my mother's idea. She said I would need to speak both, Spanish and English to be able to trade with them when I get older.

"Your mother was a wise woman. Where do you come from?"

"I come from a place called, California. I have traveled far. I am from the Luiseno tribe. My father was a sub-chief and my mother was Mexican."

Clay let out a low whistle. The boy had done well, traveling so far, all alone. He had sand - that was for sure. But the truth was, he was still just a boy.

Clay reached across and stuck out his hand. My name is Clay Brentwood you can call me, Clay. What should I call you? I hate not knowin' ah man's name when we're talkin'."

The boy smiled and said, “I am not yet a man I have a man’s job to do. I am called, Adam Castillio Cahuilla you can call me by either my Christian name, Adam, or my Indian name, which is, Little Frog.”

“I kinda like Little Frog,” Clay said with a grin as they shook hands.

“I like that too,” the boy said, grinning widely.

For the next several days, Clay almost wished the boy hadn’t decided to talk. He never seemed to run out of things to talk about or questions to ask.

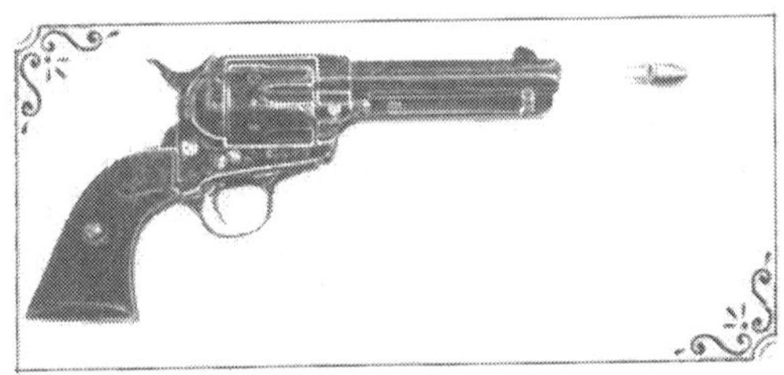

CHAPTER THIRTY

Clay was nine days southeast of Antelope Wells, somewhere between four hundred and fifty and five hundred miles south of the border and he was feeling the fatigue caused by blistering sun and sitting in the saddle day after day. His lips were dry and cracked and his patience was on edge. It sort of irritated him that the boy didn't seem to be bothered by the trip and was singing a song about being a warrior and having courage, as he set easily on the back of the steel-dust, riding without a saddle. Clay had given him a blanket to lie across the horse's back to keep it from getting sores. The boy seemed to like the blanket and the steel-dust didn't seem to notice the small amount of weight on his back.

It was late in the afternoon, and Clay was looking for a place where they could make camp when he saw the spiral of smoke in the distance. It was between them and some ancient volcanic hills further to the south. Hauling on the reins of the black, he pulled him up short. The boy rode up next to him and asked, "What does that mean?"

Clay rubbed the stubble of beard on his chin and said, "If it means what I hope it means, we're about to go to war."

The boy's eyes got wide with excitement. "War? Si, Senor', I am ready. But how do you know that it is them?"

"I've been seeing fresh wagon tracks for a couple of days now and I figured it would just be a matter of time before we caught up to them. They can't travel as fast as we can."

"What can I do, Senor' Clay?" the boy asked with excitement in his voice.

Clay turned and looked at the boy and for the hundredth time, wondered how he could go about rescuing the women and keep the boy safe at the same time. "I really don't know," he said in all honesty. "Once I figure out ah plan, I reckon the best thing you can do is to stay hidden until I do what needs ta be done. Maybe you can watch the horses or somethin'."

Little Frog's face went from smiling to a look of anger. "No, Senor'. I did not travel all this way to hide in the shadows like a whimpering child while someone else rescues my sisters. No Senor'. I will do my share of whatever the plan is."

Clay looked at Little Frog, sitting tall and determined astride the steel-dust and realized the boy was becoming a man much faster than should be; but life out here was hard. You either survived or you didn't.

He had to respect the boy's tenacity and daring. He may be young he was brave and was on a mission. He'd already proved that by coming so far, alone.

"Very well," Clay said. "We'll get closer so's we can get a look at what we're up against, and then we'll figure this thing out, together."

The boy smiled and stuck out his hand. Clay reached across and shook the boy's small hand and was surprised in the strength of the boy's grip.

A short time later, Clay tethered the animals in the shade of a small group of trees near the bottom edge of a hill, and then he and Little Frog made their way to the crest of the ridge and cautiously, peered over.

They were surprised to see another stand of trees next to a small lake, which was probably fed from an underground river coming out of the nearby mountains. Clay lifted his field glasses to his eyes for a closer look.

The prison wagon sat out in the open, just beyond the edge of the stand of trees, while the camp itself was located closer to the lake and within the protection of the small forest. Female voices carried on the wind and Clay swung the glasses in the direction they came from.

A hundred feet or so from the camp, hidden by the trees, was a small inlet and it was there the voices were coming from. The women were bathing, washing clothes and seemed to be enjoying themselves. From what Clay could see, there seemed to be no guards standing around, leering at them. They were like schoolgirls on an outing, and they were all young, very attractive and naked!

Clay counted fourteen young women. Some were jumping around, splashing each other and laughing, while others were swimming in the cool water. Three of them were doing laundry. Clay hated to stare to see them like this was mesmerizing. He was only able to lower the glasses when the boy asked, "What do you see, Senor'?"

"It's them, alright," Clay said, not mentioning the fact that he'd just seen the boy's sisters, completely naked. "They've got a camp down there in the trees and the women folk are off to the side where the men can't see'em and they're takin' ah bath and washing their clothes. Probably the first time since they were taken captive," Clay said.

"How do you know they are taking a bath, Senor' Clay? Can you see them? Did you see my sisters?" Little Frog's look of concern caused Clay to take care in the way he answered the boy's questions.

"I can hear water splashin' and hear their laughter; so I'm just supposin' that's what they're doin'. It just kinda makes sense."

Little Frog thought for a moment, then nodded his head; satisfied that his sister's integrity had not been abused.

"So, do we ride down and shoot the bad men and rescue the women like they do in the dime novels?" he asked after a moment.

Clay shook his head from side to side. Dime novels were for certain, givin' folks the wrong impression of the west. "No, that's not how it really works. We'd probably wind up getting ourselves killed, which wouldn't be any help to the women, now would it?"

Little Frog got a disappointed look on his face and said, "When you put it that way, I guess you are right, Senor'. So, what do we do?"

Clay slid back down the hill far enough so he could stand up and walk back to the horses. Standing next to the black stallion, he stared at the sky.

"There's an idea forming in the back of my mind I need ta think on it some and maybe toss some ideas around before I come to ah decision.

Here, have ah piece of jerky while I ponder on this idea," he said, reaching into his saddlebag for the jerky.

How he was going to do this, he was still not sure. But one thing was for certain, it would have to involve the boy or he would be insulted and Clay didn't want to do that. It had to be something the boy would feel he was a part of, yet keeping him safe and at the same time, get the women out of harm's way, along with somehow doing away with the men who started this whole thing.

Going in with guns blazin', was one way – a reckless way – plus there would be a lot of bloodshed the boy really didn't need to see, and the possibility of some of the women getting hurt.

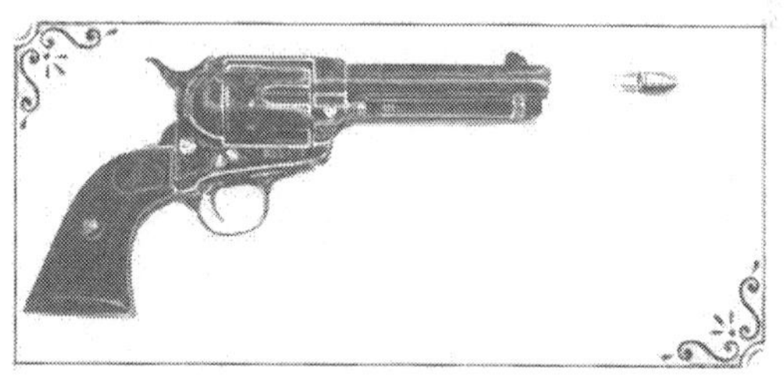

CHAPTER THIRTY-ONE

-

Fortunately, for what they had to do, the moon was hidden behind a very large, dark cloud that was moving slowly across the sky, giving them time to at least get the party started before the slavers came full awake.

Little Frog stood near where the horses were picketed, after Clay made sure the man guarding them was taken care of.

"You know what to do?" Clay asked.

"Si, Senor'. You do not need to worry about me, I will be ready when you are," he said, and then silently headed toward the prisoner wagon.

While Little Frog was making his way toward the wagon, Clay crept close to where the men were sleeping - yet still hidden within the forest, where he waited.

Little Frog crept up next to the wagon and spoke softly, calling out his sister's names.

She Who Sings pushed her face against the bars; eyes wide, an astonished look on her face. "What are you doing here?" she hissed. "Go away! These men are very bad and will not hesitate to kill you!"

Little Frog gave her an exasperated look and shook his head. "I am not alone. My friend and I have come to rescue you and take you home. Now be quiet and listen."

By then several faces were pressed against the bars.

"Where do they keep the key to the lock?" Little Frog asked.

A girl by the name of Betty spoke up first. "On the other side of the wagon; it's hanging on a hook."

"I will unlock the door you must be very quiet and do not try to get out of the wagon until I tell you to."

When he could see that they were all shaking their heads, he made his way to the other side of the wagon where he found the key and then very quietly, slipped the key into the lock and turned it slowly. At the crucial moment, Little Frog made the sound of a bird fluttering its wing at the same time the lock made a slight click sound as it dropped open, then, making no other sound, he disappeared into the trees.

The women in the wagon were tempted to open the door and try to escape Little Frog's sisters intervened, whispering to them that Little Frog was their brother and could be trusted. "If he says we should wait, he has a reason, so please do as he says," Pretty Bird, said.

Although they were nervous, they sat down and leaned their backs against the bars of the wagon, each one praying they were doing the right thing. But the truth was, even if they were to escape, where could they go that the slavers could not find them. And when they were found, what would happen then?

Clay waited until the cloud passed by the near full moon, and when the area lit up almost like day, he yelled, "Alright boys we've got'em surrounded! Don't open fire unless I give the word!"

At the sound of Clay's voice, the slavers jerked awake, sat up, grabbing for their guns, looking around - trying to find someone to shoot at there was nothing but the darkness of the trees staring at them.

Clay stepped into view and yelled, again, "Stay well-hidden men and remember, no shooting unless I give the word."

To the slavers, he said, "Toss your weapons over toward the fire, then roll over on your stomachs and put your hands above your heads and nobody will get hurt."

Most of the slavers complied without hesitation. But one of them sat where he was and looked around. He was a tall man, dirty, unshaven, with a wicked mouth and mean looking eyes that stared hard at Clay. When he saw no one but Clay, he said, "Mister, I don't see anybody but you. How do I know you're not blowin' smoke? Maybe you're here all alone and tryin' ta fool us."

Without hesitation, Clay called out, "Zeb, am I here all by myself?"

An instant later a rifle sounded from the opposite side of the camp and a bullet scattered dirt just a few inches from the man who had questioned him.

The man tossed his pistol toward the fire, rolled onto his stomach and reached his hands above his head.

"Okay, I believe you!" the man said, pushing his face against the ground.

Little Frog held the butt of the rifle against his shoulder just like Clay had taught him to do in case he had to fire another shot. It would have been easy to kill this man who had stolen his sisters Senor' Clay had told him not to shoot anyone unless he absolutely had to.

"Keep'em covered," Clay yelled as he walked forward, thankful that Little Frog hadn't shot the man. He knew Little Frog hated these men and he wanted revenge. "Anybody moves, shoot to kill," Clay yelled in the direction of the forest as he walked up next to the fire.

Within five minutes, all the slavers were bound with pigging strings and their gun rigs were stacked in a pile near the fire.

Clay squatted near the fire and poured himself a cup of coffee and blew on the hot liquid before he tasted it. But when he did, it tasted mighty good. Somebody knew how to make coffee – must have been one of the women.

When Clay was satisfied they were secured, he yelled out. "One of you boys go release the women and then gather up the horses!"

Little Frog lowered the rifle and giggled. That would be him. Senor' Clay's plan had worked to perfection. He is a smart man, this Senor' Clay Brentwood, Little Frog thought to himself as he raced through the trees in the direction of the wagon.

Shortly, Little Frog and the women came walking into the camp.

Seeing the guns laying near the fire, several of them wanted to grab them and shoot the slavers. It was only Clay's commanding voice that saved the slavers from being executed where they lay.

"Don't even think about it. I know they deserve to be punished for what they did, and they will hold off for now."

One of the young women, a tall, brunette who looked as though she'd been to hell and back, stared hard at the pile of guns.

"I reckon you have every right to think what you're thinkin," Clay said to her, "but trust me when I tell you, they'll get what's comin' to them."

In all honesty, Clay couldn't blame the women for how they felt. In their place, he may have wanted to do the same thing; in fact, he was sure he would.

After a long hesitation, the woman turned her head and looked toward the sky, tears streaming down her cheeks, making dark stains on her dirty face.

Over the first good meal the women had had in some time, Clay explained finding the Senora and the other two ladies and how they had helped to put him on the trail of the slavers, along with piling praise on Little Frog for his bravery.

Both his sisters were sitting next to him, proud of their younger brother.

"I knowed it. Damn my eyes!" the unbelieving slaver yelled at the top of his voice. "We've been hoodwinked like ah bunch of schoolboys." His eyes were flashing daggers at Clay. "You and thet snot nosed kid may have got the best of us this time the next time you won't be so lucky."

Clay scratched the back of his neck and said, “The way I see it, there won’t be ah next time.” He couldn’t let the man see how amazed he was that the plan had actually worked. It had been a long shot and they’d been lucky right now the only thing he could think about was, it had worked and they had captured eleven very bad men with only one shot being fired - and without killing anybody.

“What’ya mean by that,” the man asked. “What you plannin’ on doin’?”

Clay took another sip of coffee, then waved his hand toward the women, “For one thing, I could just give ya over to the women and turn my head. I’m sure they’d like that. Or, I can turn you over to the Mexican authorities, and after these ladies tell them how you treated them, well, I reckon your guess is as good as mine as to what they’ll do; maybe ah hangin’, or ah firin’ squad, which, either way, I’m thinkin is too quick ah death for the likes of you.”

“On the other hand,” Clay said with a big grin, “we could haul you back across the border and leave you locked up in the wagon, right in the middle of Apache country with the key hangin’ on the side where they could find it easy enough. I hear they like ta see how strong ah man is before he starts screamin’ and beggin’ them ta kill him.”

The slavers stared at Clay in disbelief. “You wouldn’t do that, would ya, mister?” one of them asked.

Clay smiled at them and raised his coffee cup in their direction, then took a sip of coffee without saying a word.

The truth was, Clay wasn’t sure what to do with them. As much as he wanted to, he couldn’t just walk away and leave them here, tied up and at the mercy of the wolves or other wild animals who would surely provide them with a horrifying death – an option he hadn't mentioned because as mad as the women were, he was sure that's what they would demand he do; that is, after inflicting as much pain on them as they could without actually killing them.

The sun had been above the horizon for a little more than an hour as Clay stood, looking out across country so flat you could see your next two to three days of riding.

A column of dust far to the south was rising into the open sky. It wasn't animals, Clay decided. Animals would be more spread out. No, it was a group of men and they were coming across the desert at a good pace. They were still far enough away that he couldn't be sure who they were or why they might be riding in his direction. In this part of Mexico, it could be banditos, Indians or Federales – and any one of them could mean trouble. Clay pondered on what to do. If there was to be trouble, did he turn the slavers loose and give them guns to help with the fightin? Not the best option he could think of. On the other hand, he figured the women would be willing to fight to keep from going back into captivity. But would they be willing to kill to keep their freedom? Most women had a strong notion about killing.

Clay dropped the last of the cigarette he'd been smoking onto the ground and snuffed it out with the heel of his boot, then walked over and opened his saddlebag, taking out a pair of well-used field glasses.

The women were also looking at the column of dust – anxious looks on their faces.

Propping his elbows across the back of the black stallion, Clay lifted the glasses to his eyes and adjusted them, pulling the lead rider into focus.

The rider was a proud man who rode tall in the saddle. After a moment, Clay lowered the glasses and replaced them into his saddlebag.

"Who did ya see?" the troublesome slaver asked. "Is it Indians? You wouldn't really turn us over to'em, would ya? Give us our guns back. Give us ah chance fer God's sake."

All the slavers were looking at him with fear in their eyes. To die at the hands of the Indians was a fearsome thing to think about.

The women were also staring at him.

Suddenly, Clay was enjoying himself. He smiled and said nothing as he rolled and lit another cigarette. He wanted to tell the ladies he figured everything was gonna be alright the fear on the slavers faces made him decide to wait a bit longer.

One of the slavers swallowed and said, "Look mister, I don't know who you are, or why you're here we got money, lots of it over there in our saddlebags. If you turn us loose, you'll go home ah rich man and you can keep the whores."

Several of the women started to get up Clay waved them back, and then turned and looked directly at the man. He was short, with big eyes and tobacco brown teeth. Like the rest of the slavers, he was dirty and unshaven. He had a smirk on his face that told Clay all he needed to know. There might be money in the saddlebags they'd never let him have it, nor would he get out of here alive. These were hard men, not to be trusted. They would kill him; of that he was sure.

After Clay rolled his smoke, one of the women, a pretty thing of about eighteen with long brown hair and soft brown eyes, pulled a stick from the fire and moved over close to him, and as she lit his cigarette, she said, “He’s lying. As soon as you turn them loose, the first time you turn your back, they’ll kill you.”

Clay blew a smoke ring and said, “I know, and you tell the ladies not ta worry, I’m not turning the likes of them loose, no matter what. I reckon I’d be safer in ah hole with ah bunch of rattlesnakes all wantin ta bite me at the same time.”

“Well, what’s it gonna be? You want ta be ah rich man with yer own harem?” the man yelled at Clay.

“I don’t want your money,” Clay said, shrugging his shoulders. “And as for havin ah harem, I don’t rightly see how I could handle this many women all by myself. Hell, I’d be ah dead man within two weeks.”

Clay heard several snickers from the young women, and grinned as he went on. “Besides, it ain’t up ta me. The way I understand it, the womenfolk took ah vote and they all want ta see the whole lot of ya rottin’ in hell. They said they’d be happy ta do it if I didn’t have the stomach for it.”

The slavers looked at the women – knowing that after the way they’d been treated, they could kill them and never think twice about it – and, like at the hands of the Indians, it would be a slow, painful death.

“Or, and I understand this would be their second choice; we turn ya over to the authorities and let them do it. Any way ya look at it, you boys are goin’ ta hell right soon like, so I reckon you’d better start makin’ your peace with the almighty if you’re of that way of thinkin’.”

The silence that hung over the morning was so thick you could have cut it with a knife. Not one of the slavers had anything to say several of them had their heads bowed, either mumbling a prayer, or trying to put a curse on this stranger and the boy who had suckered them into surrendering.

Little Frog walked over and looked up at Clay - excitement in his eyes. "Senor' Clay, did you see who is coming? If we are going to have to fight, I am ready."

Clay put his hand on Little Frog's shoulder and said, "It's always good to keep your gun loaded don't be too quick ta use it. I'm thinkin' the men comin' our way will be on our side."

Clay walked causal like over to where the slavers bedrolls were and began going through their saddlebags. When he'd finished, he let out a slow whistle. The man who'd said they were rich, was right, they did have money. Clay was holding several thousand dollars in his hands.

"Hey, you can't do that," one of the slavers yelled.

Paying the man no mind, he looked at the dust column and knew it would be at close to half an hour before they arrived – enough time to do what he needed to do. He walked to his horse and put the money in his saddlebags, put some wet wood on the fire to create smoke then motioned the women to follow him as one of the slavers called out, "Hey get that wet wood off the fire. Are you crazy? You're gonna bring those Indians out there right to us."

Gathering the women at the side of the wagon, out of sight of the slavers, Clay spoke to them in a casual voice. "When that cloud of dust gets here, from what I can tell it's gonna be loaded with Mexican Federales, who I hope will be on our side. I plan on turning the slavers over to them and I want you ladies to tell them who you are, how you come ta be here and how you were treated. I know it will be difficult for some of you do the best you can. If they are the kind of men I hope they are, you'll get your justice."

"And if they aren't?" one of the women asked.

Clay thought for a moment then said, "I suggest each of you go over to that pile of guns and get one. Make sure it's loaded and then hide it in a pocket if you have one. If you don't have someplace ta hide it on your person, then hide it in ah place where you can get to it real quick like."

The women looked at each other, and then followed a tall, auburn haired woman toward the pile of guns.

All the while they were doing this, the slavers watched, wondering what the women were going to do.

A few minutes later, the column of men rode up. The man in the front was a tall man with the look of a leader. By his insignia, Clay figured him to be a captain.

When the dust settled, Clay counted twenty men as he stepped over next to the captain, and looked up.

The captain's eyes roamed over the camp, taking special interest in the men tied up and then allowed them to linger on the women. "I am Capitan Jose Luis de Marcus Villages of the Mexican Federales. What goes on here? Who are those men and why are they tied up? And who are those women?"

"Those men are slavers, bound for Matamoras ta sell these women they stole from up north of the border. Accordin' to the ladies, who are not whores by the way, just innocent women who were kidnapped by these men. They also told me they have been beaten, starved and used by these men against their will.

"I was trailin'em ta get back one of the women they abducted, and I was able ta rescue her up north at Antelope Wells, ah Senora Ontiveros and two others. After seein' them headed home, at the Senora's request, I crossed the border and come lookin' for the rest of'em. I know I got no authority here when I met the boy here," he said, pointing at Little Frog, "and found out he was trail'em too.

These men kidnapped his two sisters and he was bound and determined ta get them back. Now, I figured he was ah mite young ta be goin' after the likes of these men all by himself. Figured he might need help, so we teamed up. We trailed'em all this way before we caught up to'em and then we sorta surrounded them, ya might say, and took'em prisoners."

Pointing toward the women, Clay went on. "We was just discussin' what ta do with'em when we saw your dust column. Took ah look at you through my long glasses and saw who you were, so we just waited."

At that, Clay stepped back and let the captain digest what he'd just heard. And, after a few moments, the captain stepped down from a fine looking gelding, dark roan in color who looked like he would do in a long run.

As soon as he stepped down, a corporal ran up and took the reins. The captain nodded and approached Clay.

"This will take some sorting out. Do you have any American coffee, Senor'?"

Clay grinned and said, "Just made ah fresh pot. Got some sugar if that's to your likin' no cream or milk."

"Just black," he said as he followed Clay over to the fire and accepted a cup of strong, hot coffee. "I learned to drink it that way when I was up north, going to school at a place called, Yale."

Clay let out a low whistle. "Never been there but I've heard of it. I'm impressed."

The captain smiled, pleased with Clay's reaction. After a few minutes of enjoying his coffee, he pulled out a leather container that held several dark brown cigarillos. After taking one for himself, he held out the container in Clay's direction. Clay took one and said, "Thanks."

When they'd lit up and had taken a few puffs, the captain looked at Clay and said, "Please, Senor', explain to me, again, what is going on here?"

Twenty minutes and another cup of coffee later, the captain nodded his head. You say you are the Segundo who works for Senora Ontiveros, Si?"

Clay nodded his head and said, "That's correct," wondering why he'd asked that question.

"And Senor', are you also the man who engaged in a shootout with the outlaw, Curly Beeler and his gang and killed them all?"

Clay hung his head and shook his head. Was there no place he could go where somebody hadn't heard the story?

"Yes I'm not a gunfighter, if that's what you're insinuating."

The captain raised both hands, palms forward. "Oh no, Senor'. I was insinuating nothing of the sort. I have also heard the story of why you trailed and shot these men. The Senora herself told it to me some time ago. We are friends. We went to school together.

Clay was surprised but tried not to react. “I see,” he said and let it go at that.

“I will need to speak with both the women and the prisoners before I make my decision on what to do.”

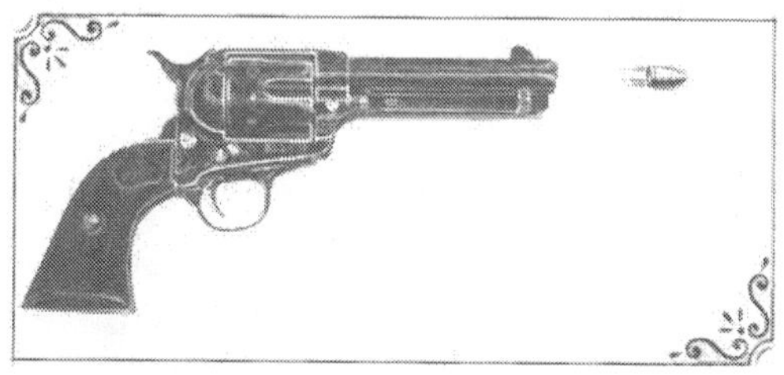

CHAPTER THIRTY-TWO

-

The captain didn't seem to notice the sergeant squatted near one of the slavers, talking in a low tone Clay did.

After a few minutes, the sergeant stood up and walked back to the soldiers and began talking to them, pointing toward Clay's horse.

The hair on the back of Clay's neck began to rise as he leaned down and told Little Frog to very quietly, take his rifle and sneak into the trees and stay out of sight.

Without a word, Little Frog disappeared into the trees.

Clay's rifle was still in the saddle-boot his pistol was loaded and hanging loosely in the holster next to his leg. Slowly, without making an issue of it, he released the thong holding the pistol in place, then walked casually over to his horse and pulled his rifle from the boot.

When he turned around, the sergeant was standing a few feet away, pointing a pistol at his mid-section. "I will have the rifle and side arm, Senor'," the sergeant said in a quiet tone.

Clay looked over toward the captain, who had his back to what was going on saw the woman with the auburn hair staring in his direction.

Clay raised the hand not holding the rifle, in the air. "And why should I give you my weapons?" Clay asked in a louder voice than he needed to.

The woman with the auburn hair said something to the captain, who turned to see what was going on. Seeing Clay with his hand in the air and the sergeant pointing his pistol at Clay, he said, "Sergeant! What is the meaning of this? Put that pistol down!"

"Juan!" The sergeant yelled, and before the captain realized what was happening he was surrounded by several of the soldiers who were pointing pistols at him.

"What is the meaning of this?" he asked as his pistol was taken from its holster.

Nodding toward the slavers, the sergeant said, "Roman is my second cousin on my mother's side and he told me this gringo has stolen all their money and has it in his saddlebags. He also said the gringo only wants the women so he can sell them himself.

If we turn them loose, we can have the money and the women."

"And you believe this man?" the captain asked.

"It makes no difference; he is my cousin. Besides, none of us has ever seen the kind of money he talks about. We will be rich and will not need to be soldiers anymore."

The captain thought for a moment, then said, "Sergeant, I order you and the others to put your weapons down, now!"

"You do not give the orders any more. I do. I will have my share of the money and the women."

At that moment, Clay yelled, "Now!" as he lowered his hand and pointed the rifle at the sergeant.

What happened next surprised not only the soldiers but also the captain.

Seemingly out of nowhere, the women produced pistols and were pointing them at the soldiers and the air was filled with hammers being cocked.

The soldiers stood there, not knowing what to do until the captain spoke up. "As I said before, you men put down your guns and maybe you will not die, today."

The air was tense. Clay was holding his breath. His finger rested on the trigger of the rifle.

Just when it looked like the soldiers were going to put their guns away, Ramon yelled out, "What's the matter with you? You afraid of a bunch of skirttails? Kill'em all!"

The sergeant raised his pistol and at the same time, Clay squeezed the trigger on his rifle. Blue smoke exploded from both weapons Clay's shot was not jerked as was the sergeants. The sergeant was lifted from his feet and driven backward when the bullet slammed against his chest. At the same time Clay fired, he moved slightly to his left, which saved his life. The sergeant's bullet barely singed the side of his neck as it went harmlessly into the trees.

But those two shots were enough to start the dance. As the soldiers turned their guns toward the women, the women cut loose and the air was filled with blue smoke and the sound of pistols being fired.

Nine soldiers had dead eyes staring at the sky, while three others were sitting on the ground, bleeding from wounds inflicted by the women. The rest had dropped their guns and stood with their hands in the air.

Little Frog stepped from the trees, the rifle against his shoulder, ready to fire if he needed to. Clay noticed smoke still coming from the end of the barrel and wondered if he had actually killed anyone. He hoped not. The boy was too young to start killin'.

The men, who had given up, confessed they had just been taking orders from the sergeant. They were not charged with treason and remained as they had been, soldiers of the Federales.

The question of the money had also been cleared up.

"Yes, I have the money I don't plan on keeping any of it. I plan to divide it among the women. Figure they deserve it after what they been through. Besides, the slavers ain't gonna need it where they're goin'," Clay said with a slight smile.

"And where is that, Senor'?"

"Hell," Clay said, staring into the captain's eyes.

"And the women?" the captain asked.

"I plan on deliverin' them back, safe and sound, to wherever they come from."

"That is what I was hoping to hear, Senor'. After what the Senora said about you, I would expect no less. Now, what to do about the slavers?"

At that point the woman with the auburn hair stepped up next to the captain and whispered in his ear.

The captain stared into the sky as if making a difficult decision. Finally, he turned to his men and ordered them to stand the slavers up with their backs facing the woods.

When that was done, he walked back and forth, speaking with an authoritative voice. "Here in the field, it is sometimes my duty to act as judge and jury and even executioner. After hearing from the ladies and witnessing your behavior, it is time for me to make a decision.

Finally, near the center of the line of men, he stopped. "I do not have enough men to safely transport you all the way to Matamoras, where the authorities may or may not do what needs to be done. After all, they were more than likely looking forward to various rewards from your endeavors."

The slavers, still with their hands tied behind their backs, were looking at each other. "What the hell you talkin' about, Captain?" one of them asked. "What kind of favors? We don't do favors fer nobody."

The captain smiled. "Yes, I expected you to say something like that. Your lying has only helped me make my decision."

"And what might that be?" one of them asked. "You actual ain't got no authority ta do anything but take us inta Matamoras and turn us over to the law there, right?"

Suddenly, the line was filled with voices agreeing with their fellow slaver. It was a way to get out of their predicament and possibly go free.

Clay stood next to his horse and watched the proceedings, wondering what the captain had in mind. What the slavers didn't realize was, this was Mexico, not America and the laws weren't the same down here.

The captain stood, staring at the slavers for what seemed an eternity before he said, "It is my decision that you are guilty of kidnapping, bringing women across the border against their will, abusing them for your own pleasure, with the plan to sell them into slavery, whatever kind that may be."

Suddenly the men got very still.

"Your penalty will be death by a firing squad, here and now. Do any of you want blindfolds?"

When none of them said anything, the captain said, "Very well." then nodded toward the women, who were now holding rifles in their hands.

When the women walked over next to the captain and faced the slavers the captain turned and looked at Clay. "Their vote was unanimous."

Clay nodded that he understood what surprised him most was when Little Frog walked over and stood next to his sisters, holding his rifle in his right hand.

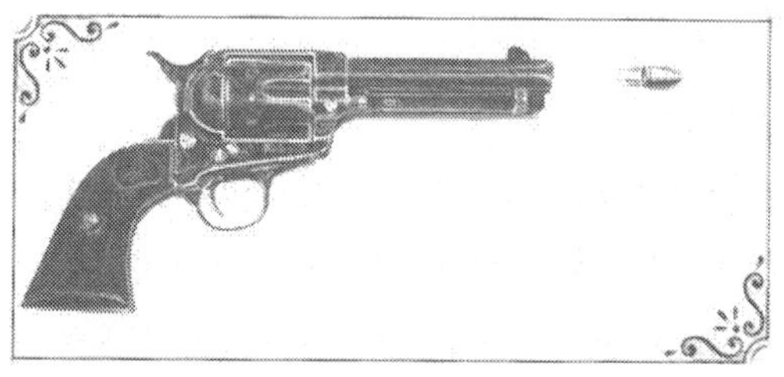

CHAPTER THIRTY-THREE

-

Two weeks later, Clay stood on the platform at the train station in Albuquerque, New Mexico, saying goodbye to Little Frog and his two sisters.

After splitting the money he'd taken from the slaver's saddlebags with all of the women, who insisted Little Frog get an equal share, he had seen each one of the women home, safe and sound.

When Little Frog's sisters came up to hug him for what he'd done, he sighed a big sigh of relief. They were the last. He'd never been hugged and kissed so many times in his life. And all of them had sworn they would never forget him. The tall woman with the auburn hair had been the worst. She'd offered much more than thanks.

Clay had thanked her and told her he was honored he was already spoken for, which was not entirely the truth it got him out of a sticky situation.

Now there was only Little Frog, who stood looking at him. After a long moment, Clay stuck out his hand. Little Frog was about to shake his hand then rushed over and hugged Clay. "Thank you, Senor' Clay. Not only did you help me save my sisters also, you have taught me what it means to be a man. If you are ever in California, mi casa es su casa; my house is your house."

Clay stood the boy back and held him by the shoulders. "It is I who should thank you. I could not have rescued them without your help."

"Si, we make the good team. Yes?" the boy said, grinning from ear to ear.

They looked at each other for a long time before Little Frog said, "I must go now, my sisters are waiting." And with that, he turned and ran for the train, not wanting Clay to see the tears forming in his eyes.

It was only when the train had disappeared beyond the western horizon that it finally sunk in. He was finished. He'd done what he'd set out to do and now it was time to go home.

That evening he treated himself to a bath and a shave and clean clothes – along with a couple of drinks and a good night's sleep.

The following morning, Clay found himself astride the black stallion, wondering where home would be? Should he go back down to the Senora's ranchero and his job as Segundo, or, should he head east and go back to his ranch in Texas? He really didn't actually need to go back to the ranchero other than to say goodbye. He'd heard Ramon had recovered and was doing a good job as Segundo.

Putting his heels lightly against the stallion's sides, he decided to let the horse help him make the decision. At the edge of town, Midnight, as Clay had come to calling him, turned onto the road heading south toward the Senora's ranchero.

About the same time Clay and the black stallion headed south, a tall, lanky man with a bushy mustache, wearing a worn suit walked into the hotel and headed straight over to the clerk. "My name is Captain Bill McDaniel; head of the Texas Rangers and I'm looking for someone who is possibly staying here in this hotel. His name is Clay Brentwood. I got paper on him."

THE END

MEET THE AUTHOR

JARED McVAY is a four-time award-winning author. He writes several genres, including - westerns, fantasy, action/adventure, and children's books. Before becoming an author, he was a professional actor on stage, in movies and on television. As a young man he was a cowboy, a rodeo clown, a lumberjack, a power lineman, a world-class sailor and spent his military time with the Navy Sea Bees where he learned his electrical trade. When not writing you can find him fishing somewhere, or traveling around and just enjoying life with his girlfriend, Jerri.

THANK YOU FOR READING!

If you enjoyed this book, we would appreciate your customer review on your book seller's website or on Goodreads.

Also, we would like for you to know that you can find more great books like this one at

www.SixGunBooks.com

Stories so real you can smell the gunsmoke.™

Made in the USA
Columbia, SC
26 February 2019